Two Reasons to Be Single

Emily Walters

Two Reasons to Be Single

Published by Emily Walters

Copyright © 2019 by Emily Walters

ISBN 978-1-09952-216-1

First printing, 2019

www.EmilyWaltersBooks.com

PRINTED IN THE UNITED STATES OF AMERICA

Dedication

I want to dedicate this book to my beloved husband, who makes every day in my life worthwhile. Thank you for believing in me when nobody else does, giving me encouragement when I need it the most, and loving me simply for being myself.

Table of Contents

CHAPTER 1 1

CHAPTER 2 16

CHAPTER 3 23

CHAPTER 4 31

CHAPTER 5 43

CHAPTER 6 55

CHAPTER 7 82

CHAPTER 8 99

WHAT TO READ NEXT? 118

ABOUT EMILY WALTERS 121

ONE LAST THING..122

Chapter 1

"What in the world?" Olivia Parker asked in astonishment as she picked up a strand of burnished orange hair cautiously between two fingers. The particular shade of orange she now held would never qualify as any sort of natural hair color.

"Can you fix it?" Joanna Bonner, one of Olivia's clients, bit her lip as she peered at Olivia from her seat in the salon chair.

"Were you going for blonde...or red?" Olivia inquired. She hoped that she wasn't offending Joanna, but in order to figure out the next step in trying to fix this mess, she really needed to know what Joanna had been trying to accomplish.

"Strawberry blonde," Joanna said sheepishly. "I followed the instructions on the box, but when I went to rinse the dye out, it looked like this." She gestured wildly to the garish tresses that hung well past her shoulders.

Olivia combed carefully through Joanna's damaged hair as she contemplated the best way to handle getting the crazy color under control. After a few moments, she knew what she was going to have to do.

"So, you want your hair to be strawberry blonde? I think I can make that happen. I'll apply a semi-permanent color and a toner, too, but you'll need to come back in about three weeks.

"The semi isn't as harsh as the permanent color, which is good because your hair can't take the permanent stuff right now; but that means the repair job will only be a temporary fix," Olivia explained.

"Do whatever you need to do, Olivia. I trust you," Joanna's voice quivered. She was on the verge of tears.

Why do people attempt to color their hair with stuff they pick up from the grocery store? Olivia thought as she ducked into the salon's back room. It was going to take a few minutes to prepare the hair dye and toner mixture she would need to apply to Joanna's cartoonish hair.

Olivia scooted past Hallie, her friend and coworker, sitting at the small break table near the back door. Lynn's Hair Salon, where Olivia had rented a chair for the past ten years, was situated in one of the original 19th century buildings on Main Street. Located right in the heart of Morning Glory, a tiny town in North Carolina she'd called home since the day she was born, the old structures had a layout that was charming but not all that functional.

Generally, when customers first entered the boutique-style salon, they were greeted by Kacie, the bubbly young shampoo tech/receptionist, who manned the polished wood desk across from the sitting area that consisted of two tufted velvet settees where clients were able to comfortably wait.

Just past the reception area through a large, arched opening was the main salon area that contained four stylist stations, two shampoo sinks and a row of dryers. A small doorway led to the back area that was just one big, open space, save for a tiny bathroom and an even smaller supply closet that had been converted into a dressing room for clients. These miniscule rooms were on either side of the doorway from the main shop area. That meant the mountains of supplies, the washing machine and dryer, the fridge, sink and table all shared the same space. From experience, Olivia knew that it could get crazy really quick in the back room if things weren't kept in precise order at all times.

"Looks like you're doing damage control," Hallie observed as she pushed around the remnants of her lunch while watching Olivia scour for the necessary tubes of chemicals.

"Nothing like a botched home job to throw another kink in your already wild day," Olivia murmured as she searched for the shade that she needed. Her schedule had been full but manageable before Kacie had to pencil in Joanna's emergency. Now, she would be lucky to get out of the salon at a decent hour. She sighed. Saturday was the worst day to have to work late. Especially when the salon normally closed at three.

Olivia had known this particular Saturday was going to be way busier than most since today was the middle school's annual end of the year dance. But to make it even crazier, on top of the slew of semiformal updos she had already been scheduled to style, she had the addition of Joanna's incident, several haircuts that had been worked in, and Mrs. Freeman, the church's organist, whose standing Saturday appointment for a shampoo and set was never rescheduled.

Mrs. Freeman never missed her weekly appointment, and she'd already made Olivia pencil them in her calendar for the rest of the year and the beginning of the next.

Grabbing a plastic bowl and a brush, Olivia mixed the tube of color with developer and set it on the stainless steel work table while the chemicals worked their magic. While she waited, she pulled a can of Coke from the antique refrigerator.

"Tell me about messed-up days," Hallie mused, "it's nearly four and I'm just now eating lunch. Eden will be here any minute to have her hair done, then we'll rush home to get her dressed before her date arrives, and then we've got to get them over to the school in time for the dance."

Olivia took a sip of her Coke and nodded her understanding to Hallie. It would never stop being weird to her that Hallie, who was only four years older than she was, had a daughter in the eighth grade. The fact only served to remind her that she wasn't getting any younger, and the big 3-0 was just a few weeks away.

Olivia stuck the half-finished drink back in the fridge, and picked up the bowl of hair color that was now ready to be applied. As she headed back out to Joanna, Olivia thought about how, when she was in eighth grade, she'd imagined her life as a grown-up to be much different than the way it had turned out so far.

Olivia's younger self would have never believed that she would still be single as the third decade of her life rapidly came to a close. She'd always assumed she would have been married by now, the mother of a couple of little ones. She thought she'd be spending her days running around to meet her other married mom friends for play dates and picnics in the park before her dashing husband came home from work. Then, their picture-perfect family would have a well-balanced dinner at the table, and after the kids went to bed, she and the dashing husband would slow dance to classic country songs by candlelight in their gourmet kitchen.

Olivia wistfully sighed. Time to think realistic. She'd already made her decision, and it was time to put it into practice. No more fanciful daydreams to remind her that life hadn't played out the way she'd wanted.

After she'd broken off her engagement with Kent Malcolm, her high school sweetheart, it seemed as though love simply made a point of evading her. It wasn't like Kent was a terrible guy, or she'd grown bitter, or anything like that—they simply knew it wasn't going to work. The flame went out and stayed out, and she had finally been the one to pull the plug. But since then, she'd only been on a smattering of dates, and none that had any potential of becoming anything more. Meanwhile, Kent was married and baby number three was already on the way.

She didn't get it. Olivia knew she was attractive, and as a hairstylist, being friendly and outgoing was part of the job description. Of course, the main issue was the fact that there weren't all that many available men to choose from—most men in Morning Glory were either married or engaged to be married if they were of an acceptable age for her to date. However, despite the lack of options, Olivia had still managed to keep hope alive all these years. She'd believed that there was someone out there just for her.

Until now. Last night, she had decided to pack that dream up and put it away. After a particularly horrific blind date the previous weekend, Olivia knew that she was over the whole dating scene. She was now resolving to embrace her future as a party of one, and she was going to make sure it would be a party, dang it.

"So do you have any big plans for tonight?" Joanna asked as soon as Olivia got back to her station, and started applying the hair color to her tresses.

"Oh yes—huge," Olivia said with a wink. "My DVR is full, and my nails need painting."

Joanna laughed. "So you're not dating anyone?" Of course, Joanna would ask the question Olivia was asked by almost every client that happened to take a seat in her stylist chair.

"Nope, and I'm not planning on it. I'm giving up on love," Olivia said with her tongue in her cheek. It sounded so cliché when she said it out loud.

"I know you're joking. From what I've gathered from hearing you talk over the years, you're all about finding love and all the hearts and flowers that come along with it."

"Well, not anymore. I haven't had a serious relationship in years, and I've been on a few dates, but most of my first dates never turn into second dates for one reason or another. I'm just going to quit worrying about it altogether—I'm over it.

"Instead, I'm going to finally take dance classes, and I'm planning on going to Europe in the fall. I'm about to turn thirty, and it's time for me to start living life to the fullest," Olivia told Joanna with conviction as she steadily worked on painting over the sherbet-shaded hair.

"That's a nice plan in theory, but you and I both know the truth about what will end up happening—as soon as a handsome, available man asks you to dinner, you'll be there with bells on, and I wouldn't blame you one bit," Joanna said with a wink.

Sometimes, it was frustrating how well Olivia's clients knew her from their years of visits to her chair.

"I know that's what would seem likely, but seriously, Jo, I decided last night that I just can't do this anymore. I'm taking control of my own destiny. I'm blessed with the good fortune of loving my career, and I have an awesome client base here in town.

"But, there are, like, three available guys that live around here, and I've been out with all of them. I have no intention to move, and I don't see how a long-distance relationship with anyone would work for me between my job, church responsibilities, the Junior League and classes I want to start taking—I have something going on all the time!"

"Well, as long as you are happy, that's all that really matters," Joanna said, conceding after Olivia finished her rant.

"I am determined to be happy. I've got a lot of good things going on in my life, and I'm tired of focusing on the one area that, well, isn't all that good."

"It makes a lot of sense when you put it that way, Olivia."

"Thanks, girl. Now, I need you to sit tight under the dryer for about thirty minutes while the dye works its magic," Olivia said, leading Joanna to one of the hairdryers and handing her a few magazines to help the time pass quickly.

Olivia stretched her aching back and glanced at the clock. She was counting the moments down until she would be done for the day. Only three more haircuts and repairing Joanna's debacle stood in the way of Mexican takeout, yoga pants and several episodes of her favorite show on Lifetime.

***

The next morning, as her Honda Civic zoomed at a speed well over Main Street's ridiculous limit, a frustrated Olivia bit her lip as her hands gripped the steering wheel. She despised being late for church, especially when she had the snacks for the children's program in her backseat. Before she could slip into the service, she was going to have to drop off the animal crackers and apple juice with this morning's nursery volunteers.

Of course, she didn't mind bringing the snacks. As the nursery coordinator, she made sure all of the rooms were stocked with supplies, each service had workers scheduled, and the little ones always had plenty of snacks on hand. Under normal circumstances, she wouldn't have been running so behind, but this morning, she'd slept through her alarm and, of course, she couldn't find anything to wear that didn't need to be ironed.

As she neared Morning Glory Community Church, Olivia glanced down at the classic black dress she'd finally settled on, tugging at its hem that kept clinging to her thigh thanks to a massive amount of static. It showcased her slim silhouette nicely when it wasn't clinging to her legs like plastic wrap. Pulling into a parking space near the back entrance, she turned off the car and quickly checked her reflection in the rearview mirror. Her dark brown bobbed hair looked fine, thankfully, and it only took a second to wipe the smudge of mascara that had somehow landed on her cheek when she'd applied it to her smoky gray eyes on the drive to church, and straightening the pearl necklace that had found its way into the collar of her dress was a snap.

Satisfied, Olivia grabbed the brown paper bag of snacks, her Bible and her purse, then hurried to the door as fast as her high heels would carry her. After slipping the bag into the toddler room without making too much of a commotion, she sped down the children's hallway and around the corner before stopping just inside the main foyer to catch her breath.

All that rushing around had Olivia feeling frenzied, and she could hear through the closed double doors that all was silent within the sanctuary other than Pastor John's soothing voice leading the congregation in an opening prayer. If she entered now, she would cause quite the disturbance, so she waited, looking over the announcements on the bulletin board while the minister finished his prayer.

As the piano began to play, signaling the end of the prayer and the beginning of the first congregational song, Olivia seized her chance to slip in unnoticed, but as soon as she reached for the door handle, it opened from the other side. She quickly hopped out of the way, but missing the door meant running right into the person swinging it open.

Olivia collided with what she could only tell was a distinctly male figure as her face hit his suit-jacketed chest. The man immediately reached out to steady her, his strong hands bracing her arms before she lost her balance and tipped over on her stilettos.

Disoriented, she looked up, and her eyes widened in surprise. She'd expected to see a familiar face, but Olivia didn't recognize the handsome man peering at her with concern in his bright blue eyes. He appeared to be in his early thirties with wavy dark brown hair, and he wore a tailored dark gray suit. In Morning Glory, most men wore khakis and bright polo shirts and wore their hair in some variation of a crew cut during the hot summer months—unless they were the pastor or over seventy years old. In comparison, this stranger's sleek suit and expertly tousled hair mesmerized Olivia.

"Are you alright, ma'am?" he asked in a polished, polite Southern drawl.

Olivia, though caught off guard, managed to nod before shifting out of his hold to steady herself on her own two feet.

"Fine, I just didn't see you coming in my rush to get inside," she explained. The sound of the choir singing boisterously floated from within the sanctuary.

"I'm sorry, I didn't see you there, either. I'm Jake Harper, by the way," he said as he extended his hand to shake in official greeting.

"Olivia Parker," she told him, taking his hand in hers. "If you'll excuse me, I'm running really behind this morning," she added before darting around him and into the crowded sanctuary. She hurried to her family's pew, and scooted onto the end of the crowded row by her cousin Lindsey.

She waved a greeting to her parents on the other end of the pew as Lindsey offered to let Olivia share the hymnal she was holding. Her mother smiled sweetly in response, but her dad pointed to his watch and shook his head. Olivia made a face at him, and he winked back at her. He loved to give her a hard time whenever he had the chance.

After the singing portion of the service was over, they settled in to listen to Pastor John as he began his weekly sermon. Normally, Olivia paid close attention, and jotted down the points that stood out the most to her, but this morning, her mind wouldn't stay focused, and her thoughts kept wandering to her chance encounter with the man in the foyer.

Her main concern was that she found Jake Harper to be too attractive for someone, namely her, who recently decided to swear off dating. Olivia also had no idea where he came from, or why he was in Morning Glory, and it was driving her crazy. Mysteries like this didn't spring up too often in their tiny little town. Everyone knew everyone here.

As the pastor continued to speak, Olivia tried to appear nonchalant as her eyes roamed around, looking up and down the aisles to see if she could spot Jake. After a few seconds, she found him. He was sitting a few rows up and to the left with Don and Maggie Harper. He seemed to be listening intently to the sermon while seated next to the older couple. Why hadn't she realized that he was probably related to the only Harpers in town?

Because you were too distracted by his hotness, that's why, she thought. She shook her head to clear her wayward thoughts. She was going to have to steer clear of this Jake guy before she did exactly what Joanna said she would do.

Why am I automatically assuming that one, he's single and two, he would immediately fall in love with me and the only thing that would stop us from being together would be my current decision to give up dating?

Olivia continued to have a mental debate with herself and overanalyze Jake for the rest of the service, and unlike most Sundays, she was glad when church was finally over. She needed to get up, move around and stop thinking so much.

As the congregation slowly cleared out of the sanctuary, Olivia noticed an array of pinks, corals and floral patterns near the Harpers' pew as she walked down the aisle. Sure enough, the single women of Morning Glory Community Church had descended on Jake Harper like a swarm of bees.

Olivia giggled at the sight of Jake's pained expression. A mixture of panic, boredom and forced politeness was plainly visible despite his attempt to smile.

Well, she certainly wasn't about to be a member of his overcrowded welcoming committee. At least a dozen women were trying to introduce themselves at the moment, and the desperation was palpable. Olivia was now more thankful than ever that she'd decided not to worry about the ridiculous game of dating anymore. In the past, if this opportunity had arisen, she would have been in the middle of all of those blonde and brunette beauties dressed in their Sunday best, trying to stand out; and that distasteful expression on Jake Harper's face could have very well been pointed at her, too.

Since she'd already introduced herself to Jake, it wasn't a big deal to go ahead and slip out of the church, and skip right past the rapidly forming Jake Harper Fan Club waiting for their turn. Jake was at the center, looking desperate to find a route of escape.

Once she'd made her way outside of the church doors, the bright sunshine was warm on her face, beckoning her to enjoy the perfect summer day. Pushing past the myriad of conflicted thoughts and emotions that had plagued her during the service, Olivia was planning on doing just that.

Chapter 2

Granny Parker's house, where at least a dozen or so of Olivia's family members gathered for lunch every Sunday after church, was the epitome of a down-home farmhouse. Situated on several acres of land just outside of Morning Glory, the two-story clapboard house was over a hundred years old, but every Parker that had lived in the house since it was built kept it in good working order and modernized it as needed.

Of course, "modern" to Granny Parker, Olivia's spry, seventy-eight-year-old grandmother, didn't include things like cell phones, computers or a television that wasn't a big wooden box on the floor. Her kitchen appliances were a mishmash, courtesy of her motto that you shouldn't replace something that could be repaired. Therefore, the cheery kitchen was the home of a harvest gold stove from the late sixties, an off-white side-by-side fridge from sometime in the early nineties and a stainless steel dishwasher that her four children had installed for her less than a year ago.

As she stood in the kitchen waiting to pull the buttermilk biscuits out of the oven for Granny, Olivia smiled to herself, thinking about how all that dishwasher did was provide storage for her grandmother's baking pans and Tupperware. She never ran the thing.

"Alright, go ahead and get those biscuits out and put them in the bread basket while they're still hot. I'm going to call the crowd in," Granny told her, starting to untie her bright floral apron that covered her Sunday dress.

Olivia did as she was told, being careful not to burn herself on the large baking sheet full of fluffy biscuits. As she placed the pan on a wire rack to cool, her sister, Katie, bustled into the kitchen with her two children. On her hip, two-year-old Molly Anne was rubbing her sleepy eyes, while Madison, the six-year-old, kept tugging at Katie's arm, asking when would it be time to eat.

Katie shot Olivia a look that said "I'm about to lose my mind," but before Olivia could offer to lend a hand, their gentle mother scooped Molly Anne out of Katie's arms. "I'll take this little one and put her down for a nap on Granny's bed," she said as Molly Anne snuggled against her shoulder.

"Thanks, Mama. I fed her a snack as soon as we got here, so she isn't hungry right now anyway," Katie replied, stretching her sore arm that had been supporting the toddler.

As Olivia started transferring the hot biscuits into the wicker bread basket that was always lined with a country blue tea towel, Katie instructed her eldest daughter to have a seat at the kids' table, and she would fix her a plate of food in just a minute.

Now that her kids were settled, she came over to where Olivia stood steadily working. "Did you see that entirely too beautiful man at church today?" she asked. Olivia knew this was coming.

"Are you talking about the guy sitting with Don and Maggie?" she responded casually.

"Um, yeah. Was there any other man at church today that could have been categorized as beautiful?"

"You know your husband was there, right?"

"Yes, Olivia, and he's sweet, funny, the love of my life, blah blah blah—we know all that. But that guy at church today was…well, the only way I can think to describe him appropriately is…smoking hot."

Olivia rolled her eyes, but she secretly agreed. She just didn't want her meddling sister to know that. "Smoking hot? I saw him, and yes, he's not bad on the eyes, but I don't think he's worth fangirling over the way those women at church were doing when I left."

"Come on, Olivia, be honest. Yes, he is worth it. I'm surprised you didn't stick around to introduce yourself. I would have if I were you," Katie said, taking the now overflowing basket of biscuits to the table.

"I ran into him when I first arrived, and I introduced myself then, so there was no need to stick around, thank goodness," Olivia explained.

"What? Why didn't you say something? What's his name? Did you find anything else out?"

"His name is Jake Harper, and no I didn't find anything else out. I was already running late, so it's not like I had time to chat."

"Even his name is hot."

"You're shooting for a new level of ridiculous, you know that, right?"

"I'm trying to live vicariously through my beautiful, single sister and you're not being cooperative!" Katie teased.

Olivia burst out laughing at her sister's silly reasoning.

"Well, I hate to disappoint, but I'm not interested in Jake Harper. I'm hanging up my hat, so to say, as far as dating goes," Olivia told Katie once she'd regained her composure.

"What are you talking about?" Katie asked in confusion.

"I'm over being disappointed. My birthday is right around the corner, and I'm taking control of my thirties. The twenties were all about getting established, trying to settle down, but it never happened. Thirty is my turning point—I'm going to focus on the things I have the ability to change."

"But…you can't control everything—that isn't any way to live life," Katie countered.

"Actually, it's much more appealing than waiting around for a guy to sweep me off my feet. I've waited a long time for that to happen, and I'm not waiting anymore. Period."

Olivia didn't give Katie a chance to respond. The rest of the family was piling into the kitchen and taking seats in the mismatched collection of chairs around the rustic pine table, and Olivia followed suit.

Katie started making a plate for her daughter, but Olivia caught the look of concern Katie shot her way when she didn't think Olivia was looking.

Olivia had a feeling no one was going to understand her decision, so maybe it was best, from this point forward, if she just kept it to herself.

***

The bright, sunny afternoon was starting to wane into a mild evening when Olivia finally left her grandmother's house. She'd originally planned on leaving much earlier, but she'd dozed off in Granny's backyard hammock where she'd only intended to spend a few minutes soaking in the warmth of the day.

An hour and a half later, the buzz of a bee nearby had awakened her from her nap. She'd been surprised when she'd taken a peek at her phone and realized the time, and now, as she pulled out of the drive, she still felt a little groggy. That was the thing about naps, a short one was always refreshing, but a long one left her tired and sleepy.

Mulling over her day, Olivia couldn't believe all anyone had wanted to talk about at lunch was Jake Harper. She'd found out from various family members that he'd just moved to Morning Glory, and Don, his uncle, had hired him as the project manager for his booming construction business. Don Harper was the best building contractor in a fifty-mile radius, so it made sense that he needed someone to help him handle it all.

Olivia's dad said that he'd heard Don wanted to eventually hand the business over to his nephew, since he and Maggie didn't have any children of their own.

Granny Parker had even commented on "what a looker" he was. The whole time, Olivia had tried to contribute as little as possible to the subject. She didn't want to give her family any ideas. They were so quick to try and set her up with any single man they could find. She knew they had good intentions, but it still didn't change how frustrating it was.

At least, Katie hadn't said anything in front of the family. Katie had kept uncharacteristically quiet during the meal, to the point that their mother had asked if she wasn't feeling well. Olivia thought Katie was probably just trying to figure out why any unmarried person would ever voluntarily decide to not date.

But it wasn't Katie's problem—Olivia was navigating her life the best way she knew how. Protecting her heart meant pushing romantic ideas away. How could she ever learn to be content with her life if she was always yearning for a relationship?

Olivia wasn't going to dwell on her decision anymore. She also wasn't going to talk about it with anyone else either. Olivia didn't want pity, disappointment or concern from others. This wasn't about them, it was about her.

Chapter 3

Back in the salon bright and early Tuesday morning, Olivia hummed as she straightened the tools and products at her station in preparation for the day. She'd spent her Monday off organizing and making plans for her ever expanding future and all of its possibilities, and the planning had energized her like nothing else could have done. She had a real zest for life, and was ready to seize the day and any opportunities it presented.

In an attempt to get started with her new lease on life, the previous morning she'd booked the trip of a lifetime to tour Europe in the fall. The vacation was going to use up a good chunk of her savings, but it would be well worth it. Olivia also signed up to take salsa dance classes in Kenton, the next town over, and ordered *The Barefoot Contessa Cookbook*, because she was determined to improve her lackluster cooking skills. The anticipation of all these new experiences had Olivia buzzing with excited energy.

Now, she just needed to figure out what to do for her thirtieth birthday that was steadily inching closer and closer with each passing day. Olivia pondered the possibilities as clients started to arrive for their morning appointments. Even though she didn't have anyone officially scheduled until eleven, she'd come in when the salon opened so that she could handle any walk-in appointments.

Just as she'd settled an older gentleman in need of a trim in her chair, the bell above the door jingled. She heard Kacie's warm greeting, and as the customer spoke, she tried to recall where she'd heard the familiar male voice.

"Hello, I'm here to meet with Lynn, she's expecting me," the strong voice said.

"Okay, sir, I'll let her know. Can I tell her your name?" Kacie asked.

"Of course, I'm Jake Harper with Harper Construction."

Olivia knew she recognized the voice from church! She swallowed hard, concentrating intensely on the silver hair between her scissors, and tried not to act like she'd noticed. Why was she letting his presence affect her? This wasn't part of her new plan or perspective.

Just ignore him, she thought to herself.

"Olivia, right?"

She whirled around at the question to find Jake standing a couple of feet away. There would be no ignoring him now.

"Hello again, Jake. Are you needing a haircut today?" she asked.

"No, I'm good right now, but I'll let you know when I do," he said, lifting a hand and running it subconsciously through his hair.

"Sounds like a plan," she said with a stiff smile before turning back to the man waiting for her to finish his haircut. For some reason, she felt awkward around Jake, like maybe the polite, but standoffish behavior wasn't just one-sided. Maybe he had issues, too.

Lynn bustled into the main room, ushering Jake to the back room as soon as she'd said hello. Maybe Lynn was finally considering remodeling the lovely, but not-so-functional salon, which would explain why Jake was here to meet with her. Olivia hoped that was the case because some sort of remodel was long overdue.

Her first scheduled client's head was covered in foils by the time Lynn and Jake emerged again from the back room.

"I'll send a couple of sketches over within the next few days so you can get a better visual of what we discussed," she overheard Jake tell Lynn as they walked past her station.

"That would be great. I'm looking forward to getting this done," Lynn replied.

"It won't take as long as you think, and we will keep the disruption to your business as minimal as possible," he told her.

Olivia watched them continue on to the front and Jake take his leave before she guided her client, Mrs. Meriwether, over to a dryer.

"Sounds like y'all are getting a renovation," Mrs. Meriwether surmised.

"I guess you were trying to eavesdrop, too?" Olivia teased her with a wink.

"I've managed to perfect the art over the course of my sixty-two years on this good green earth," Mrs. Meriwether joked.

With a lighthearted laugh, Olivia went to clean up the color bowls and unused foils while Mrs. Meriwether's hair was setting. Her heart was joyful at moments like this when she was reminded of the many relationships she'd formed with her clients over the years.

Every day, someone she knew sat in her chair and shared stories about what was going on in their life, and was genuinely interested in knowing what was going on in hers, too. Sometimes, her feet or back would ache at the end of a long, busy day, but even in those moments, she still loved what she did every day—being creative, interacting with familiar faces on a regular basis and making her clients happy. It didn't feel like work at all.

***

When the end of the work day arrived, the salon staff sat around the closed shop, chatting as they waited for Lynn to start the impromptu meeting she'd called. Olivia stretched out on one of the sofas near the front door and slid her feet out of her shoes. The day had been productive, but long, and although she wanted to know what the deal was with Lynn's plan for the salon, she was beyond ready to head home for a glass of wine and a soak in the tub.

"Okay, y'all. Thanks so much for sticking around. I know everyone is tired," Lynn said, coming out of the back. "I'll get straight to the point," she added, taking in the haggard expressions of the staff she also called her friends.

"I've hired Harper Construction to remodel the salon. We all know it's past time for it," she told the waiting women.

"That's good to hear, but how will it affect our business?" Olivia piped up, asking the question on everyone's mind.

"Jake has assured me that the renovations will be done with minimal interruptions to our day-to-day routine. We will have to close for a couple of weeks when it's time for the main area to be renovated, but it will be in the middle of the summer, which is a slow time for us anyway since everybody goes on vacation," Lynn explained, talking about the stylists' domain and the front reception area.

She went on further, going over construction specifics and how Jake and his crew would be getting started on the back area the following week. "We'll have a proper break room, supply closet and dressing area. I'll also have a decent office, too," Lynn added with excitement.

When the meeting was over, Olivia turned down Kacie's invitation to have dinner with her and a couple of her friends. She'd had a long day, and was ready to wind down and relax.

After a nice long soak, a glass of wine and a little bit of reading, Olivia slid between her cool, crisp sheets and thought about all the events and activities coming up on the horizon. She would finally be a world traveler in the fall, she would learn more about cooking and dancing, she still had her Junior League and church commitments, and now the salon was finally getting the remodel Olivia had been praying for since she'd started working there ten years ago. She drifted to sleep with a smile on her face, pleased with the direction her life was taking.

***

"I just don't get it," she heard from the row behind her. Olivia wasn't purposefully eavesdropping on the conversation taking place, but she couldn't help but hear it as she waited for the Morning Glory Junior League meeting to start.

"What do you mean?" another girl asked.

"I've dropped off a casserole, invited him to dinner, and given him my phone number, but it's like all I've gotten is the polite, but very cold, shoulder," the girl explained.

"Well, he's only been in town for a little over a week. I'm sure you aren't the only one showing him attention…maybe he's interested in someone else?"

"If that were the case, I would understand, but everyone I talk to says they've gotten the same treatment or know someone that has."

"I heard he was just being that way towards the single women that have been angling for a date," the friend pointed out. Olivia knew they were talking about Jake, and she had heard the same thing. It was a small town, after all, and people talked.

"Well, it isn't very nice. He's single, and it's a downright insult that he won't even be friends with any of us single girls. It's like we aren't good enough."

Olivia rolled her eyes and purposefully tuned out the rest of their chatter. If Jake didn't want to be bothered, that was his business. She sure as heck wasn't one of the women trying to catch his attention, but even if she were, she knew when to take a hint and leave someone alone. The rest of the women in Morning Glory, however, did not. They were completely unaware that they were sabotaging any chance of eventually dating Jake Harper by constantly throwing themselves at him.

Speaking of Jake, he was supposed to start the salon renovation project this coming Monday. Lynn had asked Olivia if she didn't mind meeting him and his crew to let them into the salon. Olivia knew Lynn felt bad asking her to do it on her day off, but Lynn had a doctor's appointment that she didn't want to cancel. Olivia had reluctantly agreed, even though spending her day in a closed salon wasn't necessarily the most appealing thought. Maybe she'd spend the time catching up on her reading or something.

Just then, Monica Hayes, the president of the Junior League, called their meeting to order, and Olivia sat at attention as she started going over their recent community contributions, putting all other thoughts out of her mind.

Chapter 4

Monday arrived, and Olivia dragged herself from her cozy bed bright and early. She stretched, trying to clear her head and push away any thoughts of resentment. Monday was the one day of the week that she had a chance to sleep late, and thanks to Lynn's doctor's appointment, she wasn't getting that luxury this morning.

Stop being selfish, she thought to herself. She was glad that this renovation was finally happening, and even if it meant a little inconvenience for her, it was still well worth it.

Not risking staying in bed a second longer for fear of lying back down on her still warm pillow, Olivia hopped out of bed and headed to the shower. She'd wanted to work out this morning, but had hit the snooze button one too many times to allow time for the gym. She made a mental note to go running this evening.

After a longer than usual shower, Olivia quickly dressed in yoga pants and a bright coral tank top. She didn't spend much time worrying with her hair, only making sure there weren't any flyaways, and she didn't put on much makeup either. Hanging out in an empty salon while a construction crew worked in the back didn't constitute an event worthy of wasting her expensive cosmetics.

Satisfied with the results of her simple beauty routine, Olivia filled a travel mug full of coffee and tossed a granola bar and yogurt in her bag. She'd eat breakfast at the shop to help pass the time.

When she parked in front of Lynn's Hair Salon after the five-minute drive from her house, Jake was already there, leaning against his big truck. As much as Olivia didn't want to admit it, Jake was the starring role in a Southern girl's daydream as he leaned casually against his pickup truck in tattered jeans and a ball cap.

He looked like the epitome of a sexy blue-collar man, from the tip of his steel-toed boots to the hint of wavy hair peeking from beneath his hat. The snug white T-shirt he wore showed off his well-cut arms, which were even more defined since his arms were folded across his chest. Olivia pushed away the inappropriate thoughts that formed too easily at the sight of him. Jake might have worn some of the most sophisticated, tailored clothes on Sundays at church, but from the look of his muddy boots, he didn't mind rolling his sleeves up and getting dirty, which made him even more appealing to her.

Why, oh why, does he have to be so cute? Olivia felt bad wishing that he was just a little less attractive for no reason other than it would make it easier for her to keep her promise to herself.

Resigning to just suck it up and look past his hotness, Olivia got out of the car and greeted Jake with a small smile and a wave.

"Hey, Olivia!" He pushed off the truck and walked up to meet her on the sidewalk. He was positively beaming, which wasn't what she was expecting. Everyone kept going on and on about how aloof he was.

"Hey, Jake. I believe I'm supposed to open up for you and your guys," Olivia replied, peering around Jake in search of his crew.

"It's just me this morning. They'll be here in a couple of hours. I'm going to get started while they finish up another job that ran over. But don't worry, it won't put us behind on this project—the other job ran over due to the client's schedule."

"I'm not worried," she said as she unlocked the door to the salon. "Just let me know what you need from me—I'll try to stay out of your way," she added once they were inside and she was turning on the overhead lights in the darkened shop.

"Thanks," he said, sounding unsure. Olivia glanced up and noticed the confused look on his face.

"Is something wrong?" she asked him.

Jake seemed to be weighing pros and cons as she waited for him to answer her. Finally, he spoke. "Well, you're just surprising me, that's all."

"What do you mean?"

"Since I've moved here, I've literally been bombarded. Overwhelmed. It's been crazy, but you're not like that. You're almost…well, not necessarily rude, but just barely on the edge of polite," he explained.

She felt her cheeks flame in anger, but she kept it in check as best she could. "Are you calling me rude?"

"No, sorry! I shouldn't have said that—it came out wrong. I meant you're treating me like a normal person would treat a stranger."

"Um, oh-kay. Whatever. Just let me know if you need anything," Olivia responded before she looked down and pretended to be busy with papers at the desk. He'd managed to get under her skin within the first ten minutes. This morning wasn't turning out so well.

He crossed the room to where she was sitting.

"You're mad at me, and I can't figure out why," he said when he'd reached the desk.

"I'm not mad at you—I barely know you," she replied, taken aback.

"You are mad. I know when women are mad."

Olivia sighed and tossed the stack of papers in her hand back on the desk. "I'm honestly not mad at *you*. I just have some…personal issues going on, but, I've also seen the way you act when women are throwing themselves at you. Don't get me wrong—I see how annoying it is, but what I don't understand is why you haven't tried to at least make friends with some of them. Despite their gushing, a lot of those girls are really nice," she explained. Olivia figured it didn't hurt to be honest with him—it wasn't like she was trying to impress him or get him to ask her out. Plus, she couldn't very well say that she was being cool with him because she *did* find him attractive, and it was frustrating her attempt to no longer worry about men and dating.

"It's for the best that I keep them at a distance. I have my own…personal issues, too, and I can't complicate that with dating. I can't be friends with any of them because I know how that goes…being friendly is mistaken for flirting, and every move I make will be analyzed." He paused before continuing, "But, you're wrong about my not trying to make friends. I'm trying to make a friend right now, but she isn't cooperating." He gave Olivia a pointed look.

Olivia couldn't help laughing when Jake held his eyebrow arched for way longer than necessary.

"Geez. Okay. I'll be your friend, but I have to be clear—that's all we will ever be—just friends. Got it?"

she asked. She didn't want to leave any doubt that she was not in the market right now for a date, just in case he changed his mind about his own resolution.

"Perfect. I'm on the same page with you," he said, smiling. "Now, I have to get to work."

"Go, do the things with the hammers and the nails and all that," Olivia said, waving him off before propping her feet up on the desk and flipping through a magazine.

The morning was trickling by at an unusually slow pace, and a couple of hours later, Olivia was about to start reorganizing her day planner for lack of anything better to do. Just as she was unzipping the turquoise leather, her phone rang. Recognizing the number, but not able to place it, she hurried to answer.

"Hello?"

"Hi, is this Olivia Parker?" a pleasant-sounding woman asked.

"Yes, it is. Can I help you?"

"Olivia, this is Hannah Carr from Rhythm and Movement Studio. I believe you signed up for salsa classes with us last week?"

"Yes, I did, and I can't wait to get started!" Olivia exclaimed.

"We're excited to get started with this class, as well. I'm just calling to get your partner's information—our receptionist forgot to get it from you when you came in last week."

"Partner information? What are you talking about?" she asked Hannah.

"Yes, your dance partner. This class requires a partner," Hannah replied.

"No one told me that, I thought we would just rotate around or something." Olivia honestly hadn't thought about it at all. She'd been on a roll signing up for stuff last Monday and it never occurred to her that she needed a partner for dance classes. She'd pictured the class being along the lines of Jazzercise or Zumba where you learned fun little steps and worked out.

"I'm so sorry, ma'am. This class, however, is Latin ballroom-style salsa dancing, and since Kenton is such a small town, we can't guarantee the number of students, or the female to male ratio. If you would like to ask someone to take the class with you, you can call me back later with their information—I just need it by the end of the week."

"Um, okay. I'll see if I can find a partner. Thanks for calling," Olivia said with disappointment. She hung up with the dance studio and resigned herself to her fate. She'd have to withdraw from the class. Where in the world would she find a partner to take dance classes with her? She'd had her fair share of work cut out for her when all she was trying to do was find a date in this town.

"Well, crap," she said aloud to the empty salon.

"That's an odd greeting," Jake said as he came from the back room where he'd been working.

"Sorry, it wasn't meant for you," Olivia told him.

"You look pissed," he observed. He made his way to the reception desk.

"This time, I am," she admitted. He kept observing her mood.

"What has your feathers all ruffled up like this?"

"I signed up for dance classes last week, and they forgot to mention that I had to have a partner for them. I mean, I should have realized that on my own, but I just wasn't thinking," she told him.

"Why don't you ask your boyfriend? Is he not into dancing, and that's what makes you so upset?"

"Way to jump to conclusions, there, Jake. I don't have a boyfriend, so his opinion doesn't exist, and therefore, doesn't piss me off."

"Oh, no boyfriend, huh? I just assumed your whole 'we will only be friends and nothing else' speech was because you were with someone."

"Did you figure that was why I wasn't fawning all over you, too? It didn't occur to you that maybe I just wasn't interested?" Of course, if she was wanting to be involved with someone, she would definitely be interested, but he didn't need to know that.

"Whoa, now who's jumping to conclusions?" he countered. "If you think that I've behaved rudely towards some of the women around town, then you're the pot calling the kettle black. You've been cold and defensive towards me since first thing this morning, and I haven't done anything to you other than sort of call you rude and assume you weren't hitting on me because you had a boyfriend."

Laughter started deep in her chest before bursting out and turning into an uncontrollable fit of giggles. She was laughing so hard that tears began to run down her face.

"I'm sorry," she managed to say a couple of minutes later as the giggles began to subside. Jake was staring at her with wide, puzzled eyes.

"I'd love to know what was so funny," he told her. Nothing in his demeanor hinted at sarcasm—he simply wanted to know.

"You just made me laugh, that's all," Olivia said. She took in a deep rush of breath that felt deliciously free after all the exercise her lungs had just exerted.

"Well, I'm glad you received so much entertainment at my expense. Now, back to fixing your problem—when are your classes?"

"They will be every Tuesday evening starting next week," she said, but silently wondered why he wanted to know.

"I'd have to rearrange my schedule just a little, but I think I could go with you. Be your partner, that is," he said, looking at the calendar on his phone.

"Wait. What? You don't have to do that, Jake. I can cancel the classes. It was my mistake, and besides, I didn't even ask you…" she trailed off.

"Oh, so you don't want to take the class anymore?"

"I didn't say that. I just—"

"So you do want to take the class, just not with me," he interrupted.

"No, that's not what I meant. I—"

"It's settled then. I'll be honest, I don't have any dance experience, but I've always wanted to learn some moves that I could break out at a party or a wedding."

She didn't know what to say. On one hand, Olivia knew that she wanted to take the salsa classes, and it didn't matter to her who her partner was. But on the other hand, Jake hadn't really given her a choice in the matter. She wasn't sure if that frustrated her, or made his take-charge but still easygoing personality more appealing.

And never in a million years did she ever think she would so easily find a willing male in Morning Glory to take ballroom dance classes with her. Most men around the area would have found it not masculine enough, or made fun of the class. That was one of the reasons Olivia had assumed it was a salsa Jazzercise kind of thing rather than paired ballroom-style instruction.

"I'm going to take you up on your offer. I really want to take the classes, but I do have one condition," Olivia said.

"What's that?"

"No more sort of calling me rude, and I'm not dating anybody or planning on it, either, so don't ask me about that kind of stuff."

"That's two conditions, but okay, as long as you do the same for me," Jake replied.

"No problem. Jake, I really do appreciate you offering to do this. It's so unexpected," she said.

"I don't mind, it sounds fun. Remember, I don't know anyone, other than my family and the guys I work with, and I don't trust the casserole parade, so it'll be nice to have something to do," he explained.

Olivia hadn't thought about that. He didn't know anyone, and she completely understood why he would be wary of all the women dressed to the nines in full makeup showing up at his door with food.

"The crew is here," Jake said, as he read a text message. "I've got to get back to business. Why don't you give me your number so we can finalize details for next Tuesday?"

She told him her phone number, and he entered it into his phone before heading back to work. When he had reached the work area, Olivia heard his enthusiastic greeting to his crew as he opened the back door for them. She smiled to herself. How could anyone have mistaken this man as being cold or aloof?

Chapter 5

The following Tuesday evening, Olivia hurried home from the salon, took a quick shower to rid the scent of hair dye and products that never ceased to stop lingering on her skin, and threw on black stretch pants and a black tank top in preparation for salsa dancing. The dress code was fairly relaxed for the dance class—the only requirements were that she must dress in comfortable clothing and smooth-soled shoes.

She'd found a pair of strappy, low-heeled black sandals at the shoe store across the street from the salon. They weren't necessarily her typical style, but they looked like the shoes she'd seen dancers wear in the Latin ballroom competition videos she'd been watching online.

Olivia heard Jake's truck pull into her little drive at precisely six o'clock. The class started at six thirty, and the studio was twenty minutes away. She swung the door open just as he lifted his hand to knock.

"Hey, Jake. How are you this evening?" she asked cheerfully, grabbing her bag and two water bottles she'd set by the door after she'd taken in his casual stance at her front door.

"Great, I hope you are, too. I guess you're ready to get going, huh?" he asked. Olivia nodded as she stepped onto the porch, pulling the door shut behind her and locking the deadbolt. She had to keep busy with these small tasks to keep herself from looking at Jake again. He was just too good-looking if there was such a thing, and her flushed face and trembling hands were going to give away her instinctual reaction to his hotness. His hair was brushed back, slightly curling at the nape of his neck, and he was wearing a black shirt and pants and dress shoes. They'd managed to match inadvertently. Everything about him, from his five o'clock shadow to the subtle scent of his soap, emanated subtle sexiness. The fact that all the sexiness seemed natural and completely unintentional only made him that much hotter.

She could no longer avoid him as he played the gentleman and held the door open for her while she climbed into his truck. As she was saying thanks, she risked a quick glance and a smile at him, and her stomach filled with butterflies, making her want to kick herself. Maybe a good kick in the pants would take her focus off of the slow, easy smile that he gave her in response as he shut the passenger door before getting in the truck and cranking up the loud diesel motor.

Olivia swallowed hard and tried to rein in her heading-out-of-control attraction to him. Maybe if she tried small talk she would get distracted from staring at the muscles flexing in his forearm.

"So what's brought you to our little town?" she asked. She flinched at how nervous and stiff she sounded.

"I...guess I needed a change of scenery. I called Atlanta my home for fifteen years, but I'm originally from Canoe Creek, have you heard of it?"

"It's about an hour from here, isn't it?"

"Yeah, it's a little bit bigger than Morning Glory, but it's at the edge of the Blue Ridge Mountains so there are a lot of vacation rentals and lodges, and a lot less locals. I left town to go to college at North Carolina State, and after college I moved to Atlanta. I visited a couple of times a year until my parents died six years ago, and since then, I haven't been back."

"I couldn't imagine moving away from here. I've lived here my whole life—the entire town has always felt like one big family to me."

"That wasn't the case for me in Canoe Creek. I felt trapped, like there had to be more to experience than just a tiny little ski town with different faces pouring through on a weekly basis."

"Well, I hope Morning Glory proves to be a family to you the way it always has for me, but I get wanting to see more of the world. I have my own trip planned for the fall." Olivia told him about her trip to Europe, and he listened and added tips from his own trip a few years back.

"Did you go alone? I'm planning to go solo on this trip," she said.

"Wow, quite the independent streak, huh? I didn't go alone."

She waited for him to elaborate, but when he didn't, she pried a little more, unable to help herself.

"So, did you go with a group of people?"

"No, I went with one other person, and that's all you're getting out of me about that." He shot her a look that said she was invading their carefully placed boundary lines.

"Okay, okay. Sorry." She should have known better, especially since she had her own things she wasn't willing to share.

They rode in a somewhat uncomfortable silence until they reached the dance studio in Kenton.

When they entered the dance studio, they followed signs directing to the salsa class, and stood on the outside fringe of the couples that had already arrived. There were a total of seven couples there to take the class, and a lovely woman, who Olivia figured was the instructor with her deep plum leotard, floral patterned skirt and perfect dancer's posture. They were all casually chatting while waiting for the official start of the class.

"Alright, everyone! For those I haven't gotten a chance to speak to yet, I'm Hannah, your instructor. Let's start out doing a few stretches and warmups to get our blood really pumping," the colorful woman instructed.

Olivia hadn't pictured the Hannah she'd spoken to over the phone last week to look anything like this woman. Olivia studied the beautiful woman with chestnut curls and sea green eyes as she began the class.

After warming them up, Hannah taught them the basic salsa steps at a quick pace. Olivia and Jake shared a look as they paused to catch their breath.

"Now that you have an idea about the basic footwork, face your partner so that I can show you one of the proper holds," Hannah told the class. Olivia and Jake faced each other and awaited further instructions.

"Okay, guys, place your right hand securely beneath your partner's left shoulder, and ladies, rest your left hand behind his right shoulder," Hannah said as she walked around adjusting elbows, posture and hand positions as needed. Olivia spread her arms out so Jake could put his hand in the right place. The pressure of his hand felt strong and secure against her back.

"Now, clasp your other hands together with your elbows at eye level and your arms at right angles," she continued. Jake held his hand out to Olivia. When their fingers touched, she felt a jolt of energy. It took every bit of self-control to keep from showing her surprise.

"Everyone, look at this couple's frame. If I didn't know any better, I'd think they'd been salsa dancing together for years. What chemistry!" Hannah exclaimed as she pulled Olivia's shoulders back the tiniest fraction of an inch.

Olivia blushed when Jake winked at her.

They began the simple, basic salsa step, moving backwards and forwards as Hannah called out the count.

"This is fun," Jake said with an easy smile as they moved.

"I'm having a blast, too," Olivia replied, returning the smile effortlessly.

When the class was over, they walked out into the warm evening. Dusk was beginning to settle.

"Did you want to grab dinner before we head back?" Jake asked her as they reached his truck.

"That would be great, I'm starving! Do you have somewhere in mind?" Olivia asked him.

"What about that little diner we passed in downtown Kenton?" Jake suggested.

"That will work for me."

They took the short drive over to the diner, and were seated almost immediately, since the restaurant was pretty much empty now that the dinner rush was over. As they waited for someone to take their order, Olivia fanned her flushed face with the laminated menu.

"I'm still pretty warm from all the dancing," she said.

"It was definitely more of a workout than I expected it to be," Jake admitted.

"At least it was a fun workout," Olivia added.

"I'd have to agree with you."

The waitress came over and took their orders. While they waited for their food, Jake and Olivia's conversation flowed easily, and Olivia found herself enjoying every second of getting to know him.

After dinner, Jake took Olivia home. Always the gentleman, he shut his truck off after he pulled into her driveway, and was about to open his door when Olivia put her hand on his arm to stop him.

"You don't have to walk me to the door, Jake," Olivia told him when he turned to see why she was keeping him inside the truck.

"I want to walk you to the door, but even if I didn't, you still deserve to be walked to the door, so yes, in fact, I do have to walk you to the door," he told her, his voice sounding low and sultry in the dimly lit truck cab.

"I just meant, you know, this isn't a date, so I don't expect things like this. I also don't expect you to pay for dinner," she said pointedly, the memory of the diner moment still fresh.

"Is it wrong to say that I enjoyed tonight more than any date I've been on in a long time?" he asked her frankly. The light in the cab completely faded out just then, but not before Olivia saw the look in his eyes. She knew that look, and it waged a complicated war within her. His eyes gave away his desire for her, which caused excitement to shiver down her spine, but it wasn't the plan. This wasn't part of her plan!

His question still lingered unanswered within the dark interior, just as her hand still lingered on his arm. She didn't know what to say—what she wanted to say and what she knew was best for her were two entirely different subjects. But before she could get a single word out of her mouth, he leaned across the middle seat and touched his lips softly against hers.

Olivia's conflicted thoughts melted away as she closed her eyes and kissed him back, reaching up to touch the curl of hair at his collar. She'd always wanted to do that. Jake slid his arms around her waist, pulling them closer together, his mouth growing more insistent as the passion between them ignited.

She reveled in it, enjoying every second of his lips molding against hers, sighing when he broke away from her mouth to trail kisses down the length of her neck, his five o'clock shadow deliciously tickling the sensitive skin at the hollow of her throat.

Her body, her heart, her everything—craved more.

And that wasn't good.

"Stop," she breathed, the command not matching her low, honeyed voice. But clearly, Jake was a gentleman because he tore his lips away from her collarbone as she placed her hands softly against his chest.

"I'm sorry, Olivia. I guess I got carried away in the moment," he said, his voice strained as he still held her in his arms, unwilling to let her go just yet.

"No, it's okay. I was guilty, too," she reminded him before using every ounce of willpower within her to wriggle out of his arms, sliding over to open the truck's door.

He hopped out to walk her to her door, staying close but not touching her. The air between them now hung heavily with an awkward tension. Olivia wasn't sure what to say or do. Of course, she'd enjoyed kissing him, but she didn't want to go down this road again—the road that had led to her decision to avoid dating. Jake had said he had reasons for not wanting things to get complicated between them, too, and now their entire world was a complicated mess.

She blew out a breath of air in frustration. "Jake, I'm so mad at us right now. I don't need another messy are-we-friends-or-are-we-more kind of relationship. I want and *need* a good guy friend. Just a friend. Plain and simple. When feelings and kissing and all that gets added to the mix, it eventually leads to someone getting hurt and the relationship ends," Olivia blurted out. He needed to know how she was feeling.

He nodded emphatically. "I completely agree with you. I was just racking my brain on how to make this situation better, and I'm so glad that you cleared the air. I really like being around you, Olivia, and I have so much…other stuff…going on in my life right now that if we were more than friends, I know I would end up messing it up," he replied. "I loved kissing you, but I shouldn't have done it—I'm sorry," he added, casting her a sideways glance.

"I already told you that you didn't have to apologize, Jake. I'm glad we are on the same page, though. I think it will make it easier to just forget about what happened tonight and move on. I really like hanging out with you, too," she admitted, fumbling for her house key as they stood on the porch, the streetlight's orange glow hardly illuminating any of the space.

It was easier to say that they would only be friends than it was to feel like they were only friends. The nearness of Jake, the dark night and the memory of their kiss from moments earlier made a heady combination, and Olivia wasn't handling their intoxicating chemistry very well.

The key finally slipped into the lock and she hurried to step inside the safe barrier of her doorway. "Thank you so much for being my partner tonight, and for dinner, too," she said, suddenly feeling shy.

"I look forward to next week. Same time, right?" Jake asked with a soft smile.

"Yep, same time. I guess I'll see you at the salon tomorrow?" she ventured.

Jake took on a distant look, the warmth leaving his eyes. "No, the crew will be there, but I have...something else that I have to take care of tomorrow. I'll see you later this week," he said, stepping back as he tossed a casual wave in her direction.

She waved goodbye, but as his truck backed out of her drive, she frowned in consternation. Her curiosity aroused, she locked her door and prepared for bed, all the while various scenarios that could possibly be the root of his sudden mood change playing out in her head.

Chapter 6

She was mad. When Friday morning dawned, her first thought after she'd turned off her alarm revolved around a wistful hope that Jake would be back at the salon today. *Her first thought.* This wasn't good. She not only went to bed with him on her mind, but she got up thinking about him, too.

As she lay there, Olivia slammed her hands down on the sheets in frustration and let out a loud, huffy sigh. She couldn't believe herself. When she'd finally made a decision to move on from the roller coaster world of dating and just focus on what she could control, what did she do? She willingly fell into the arms of a way too beautiful man, that's what she did. And now, she hadn't heard a word from him since, and was starting to obsess about it. It was obvious that she couldn't deny her feelings for him anymore, and it made her angry.

"What is wrong with me?" she asked the empty bedroom as she hopped out of bed and stretched. The familiar ache in her heart, and the butterflies in her stomach only fueled her fire. The crazy mix of worry, hope, excitement and fear was the *exact* reason she didn't want to date anymore. But she couldn't stop dwelling on what had happened between them no matter how hard she tried. As she made her bed, she pondered how in the world she was supposed to handle her feelings and still attempt to be true to the new motto she'd only recently adopted. What she needed was a distraction. Something that would get Jake completely off her mind, and give her a chance to refocus her thoughts.

After her shower, as she blow-dried her hair, the perfect distraction came to mind. She turned off the dryer, set it down and darted to the bedroom to grab her phone, knowing just the right person to help make it happen. She quickly texted Kacie:

You, me and everyone we can think of—Bottom's Up at 9 tonight! Karaoke night!!!

Bottom's Up might not have been the classiest of bars, but what it lacked in finesse, it made up for in personality—a rowdy, fun time was always guaranteed. Morning Glory only had a couple of places a person could grab a drink, and Bottom's Up was hands-down the local favorite. Since every Friday night they had a silly, but hilarious, karaoke contest, Olivia could think of no better way to get her mind off her Jake complications than tequila shots and singing "I Wanna Dance with Somebody" at the top of her lungs.

Kacie's reply was instant and enthusiastic:

Girl, I'm there! It's been too long! I'll send out a group text.

Olivia smiled and sat her phone down, feeling good. She was booked solid with clients today, and she had a fabulous evening planned. In no time, she'd be able to shut her feelings down and get back to focusing on herself again.

Despite her plans, as she pulled on a pair of coral skinny jeans and a gray tank top, Jake came to her mind again. She wondered what was keeping him from the salon. Her feelings for him put aside, she was a little worried about her friend. Something had to be up—he hadn't been at the job site for two days. She wouldn't think much of it, except that his crew was in the middle of a huge renovation, and he'd been adamant to Lynn that he would be there for everything.

With these concerns still fresh on her mind, when she arrived at the salon an hour later, her first order of business was asking Lynn about Jake's missing presence.

"I've noticed Jake hasn't been here the past couple of days. Do you think he's alright?" Olivia casually asked as she set her stuff down at her station.

"Yes, he's fine. He'd already told me he had a prior commitment Wednesday and wouldn't be here, but on Wednesday, he called to let me know that he wouldn't be here for the rest of the week. He sounded so sorry about it, I couldn't be mad. Besides, his uncle has been checking in with the crew's progress every day. He told me that the renovation is actually going a lot faster than he expected, thanks to Jake's plan," Lynn said as she checked the shampoo area's supplies.

"That's great," Olivia said, forcing a smile on her lips. She was getting upset with no justifiable cause. Jake didn't owe her an explanation for his whereabouts. They were just friends. But still, a quick text explaining his absence would have been nice. Maybe she should have texted and checked on him, but she was afraid that would have been too much. After Tuesday night's dancing and kissing, she was having problems overthinking every interaction she had with him. Would a text come off like she liked him? Would he think she was clingy?

"I'm a hot mess," she mumbled under her breath.

"Did you say something?" Lynn asked.

"No," she replied. The last thing she wanted to do was dive into her tangled web of thoughts with anyone, much less her boss.

Thankfully, the day passed by in a blur of haircuts, Morning Glory gossip and friendly banter with her coworkers.

"Bottom's Up at nine—don't forget!" Kacie called out to the stylists before she headed out the door of the closed salon.

"Are you going, Olivia?" Hallie asked.

"It was my idea. My cousin Lindsey is coming, too," she told Hallie.

"I may stop by for a while, I'm not sure yet," Hallie replied.

"I'm sure we will be shutting the place down. I hope to see you there, but if you can't make it, I understand."

Olivia was past ready to let loose and have a few drinks. She was hoping friends and alcohol would give her a much-needed respite from her mind that stayed in overdrive lately.

After her last cut, she headed home to eat a light dinner and get ready for her evening out on the town. It took her a while to decide on the right outfit, but finally she settled on a short, swing-style mint dress with a girly bow in the back. She took her time getting ready, styling her hair and applying fake lashes and a peachy pink lipstick. Sliding into peep-toe, pink patent-leather heels, she was ready from head to coral-painted toes, and she just had to do a quick twirl in the full-length mirror, feeling fun, girly and pretty.

When she arrived at Bottom's Up, the bar was packed with the usual Friday night crowd. The outdoor deck was full of people, and the parking lot didn't have a single empty space. Olivia didn't let having to park along the road and trek the long walk to the door in her high heels deter her radiant mood.

Once inside the dimly lit bar, she maneuvered her way through the crowd, finding Kacie, Lindsey and the rest of her friends and acquaintances just to the right of the bar, already loud and laughing. The room was hopping, music was blasting, and girls in cutoff shorts carrying trays of shots maneuvered their way through the crowd.

"Wow, it's pretty rowdy in here tonight—even for Bottom's," Olivia remarked as she sidled up next to Kacie.

"Yeah, I agree," Kacie said as she took two shots from the tray of a passing red-headed waitress. "Here, do this shot with me. Maybe it'll help us loosen up a little more," she told Olivia, handing her the neon plastic shot glass.

The strong, sweet concoction burned its way down Olivia's throat. As one of the first karaoke songs started up, she felt the alcohol starting to take effect, and she found herself mellowing out and just enjoying the vibrant, buzzing energy of life going on all around her in every direction.

An hour later and sufficiently tipsy, Olivia belted out "Girls Just Wanna Have Fun" with her cousin Lindsey, collapsing in a fit of giggles on Lindsey's shoulder when they received a hearty round of applause and a request for an encore.

Finished with their song, she stepped towards the high top they'd claimed as their own for the evening, her eyes laughing and slightly out of breath from their impromptu dance routine.

As she took a sip of her drink, a warm and familiar hand landed on her shoulder. "Great job, Olivia," a masculine voice whispered in her ear.

Olivia turned slightly to see Jake standing right behind her, much too close for comfort. She hadn't seen him approach, and thankfully, her intoxicated frame of mind kept her a little more at ease than she would have been under any other circumstances.

"I'm surprised to see you here, Jake," she said with a flirtatious smile. He grinned right back at her.

"After the week I've had, I need a drink worse than anyone in this bar tonight. Can I buy you one, too?" he asked.

"Sure, I'd like another paloma. I'm trying to stick with tequila tonight," she said with a wink before he headed in the direction of the bar. She turned back around to find about six pairs of curious eyes trained on her. She shrugged her shoulders at them all as she peered over the rim of her nearly empty drink.

"He has the hots for her," Kacie shouted over the music to the rest of the table when Olivia wouldn't say anything.

"Oohs" and "ahhs" and suggestive phrases were tossed around, but Olivia denounced Kacie's statement.

"We're just friends," she said as she felt her face flush with color, knowing no one at the table actually believed her.

Before risking the uncomfortable embarrassment that would surely ensue when Jake arrived back at the table with their drinks, she went to find him instead. After spotting him at the edge of the bar waiting, it took a moment to make her way over to him through the crowd.

"Hey there," she said as she moseyed up beside him, bumping her shoulder against his arm in a friendly way.

"Hey there, yourself," he replied, winking at her. "I think you are well on your way to getting rip-roaring drunk," he added.

"To repeat a good friend of mine's wise words from earlier, 'I need a drink worse than anyone in here.'"

"I promise you, I'm going to catch up quickly. I've had a hell of a week."

"I missed seeing you at the salon," Olivia said without thinking, her inhibitions considerably lowered.

"I've missed seeing you, too. I had…business to take care of out of town. Hence, the stress."

"Sorry you're stressed."

"It's alright. Definitely not your fault."

The bartender brought over their drinks, and Jake handed Olivia her pale pink one.

"That looks incredibly girly," he pointed out before taking a sip of his beer.

Olivia shrugged. "Tequila, lime and grapefruit juice—what's not to love? It's just an added bonus that it turns out so pretty," she replied, examining the drink before sipping daintily from the tiny straw.

Jake rolled his eyes, amused. "You make me smile, you know that?" he asked, leaning in close as if it was a guarded secret.

"You make me smile, too, mister," she beamed at him, her words a lot less serious than his.

Just then, the first, unmistakable guitar chords of her favorite country song filled the bar. She let out a whoop, grabbed her drink with one hand, and Jake's hand with the other.

"Let's dance," she said, more of a command than a request, giving Jake no choice but to follow her to the dance floor.

"You know, tonight you're a lot more…" he trailed off as he placed his free hand loosely on her waist.

"Relaxed?" she filled in for him as she swung her hips to the rhythm.

"I guess so. I was thinking more along the lines of wild and carefree," he told her.

"What? I'm not normally wild and carefree while I'm working or sitting in church?" she asked, pretending to pout as she turned around, pressing her body against his all in the name of dancing.

He leaned close to her ear as they moved with the music. "You look way too beautiful tonight, Olivia, and you're tempting me to do things to you that we agreed not to do."

The faint trace of a beard against her neck and his sizzling words caused a shiver to run down her spine. She closed her eyes and tilted her head back against his chest, reaching an arm behind her to pull him closer. Maybe it was the alcohol, or maybe she was finally giving in to what she really wanted.

"I don't remember making any hard and fast agreements," she said huskily, hoping he would catch her drift. His arm tightened around her waist, and she felt the evidence of the fact that he most definitely understood what she was saying.

She turned around to face him, looking up into his heated gaze, not noticing the dozens of people bumping into them on the overcrowded dance floor.

"How wrong is it that I wish we were alone right now?" she asked, biting her lip.

"Not wrong at all, if you're asking me," he said, before leaning down to kiss her, not caring who saw him do it.

Olivia clung to him, her lips meeting his eagerly, the dance steps forgotten as she got lost in his kiss.

"Do you want to get out of here?" he asked her between kisses, his lips reluctant to leave hers.

"I thought you'd never ask," she replied, looking up at him with eyes full of seductive promise.

"I'm going to settle up with the bar right now."

"I'll tell my friends you're going to take me home because I'm tired," she told him.

"Yeah, I'm sure they'll believe that's why I'm taking you home," he said, his gaze drifting to her bare shoulders and the slight hint of her breasts the strapless mint dress revealed. With those words, he let his eyes linger hungrily a moment longer before he turned around and made his way to the bar, leaving a flustered Olivia to find her friends.

She fanned herself with her hands, trying to cool down the fire he'd ignited within her. With all the concentration she could muster, she put one foot in front of the other, shimmying through the throng of bodies until she reached her friends' table.

"Jake and I are leaving, I don't feel good," she lied, announcing it loudly to anyone in earshot.

"Sure, right. I want details tomorrow," Lindsey responded, winking at her and waving her towards a waiting Jake.

"Got it. See you later," she replied, not even looking in her direction. Olivia wasn't in the mood for chitchat when a tall, chiseled Jake was staring steamily at her from a few feet away.

He grabbed her hand and led her out of the crowded bar and into the warm night. Olivia vaguely noticed that the ink-colored sky was awash with thousands of twinkling stars.

"Where did you park?" he asked her.

"Like a million miles away," she frowned.

"Me too. I was hoping your car was closer to avoid you and your heels having to pretty much walk across a pasture to get to my truck," he explained, pointing to her feet.

"That's not a big deal, I'll just take them off," she said, starting to lean down, but he held out an arm to stop her.

"I have a better idea. How about a piggyback ride?" he asked.

"If you had to park as far away as I did, that's a pretty good stretch to have to carry someone," Olivia warned.

"Are you questioning my strength?" he asked, his eyes laughing.

"No, not at all," she said, taking the opportunity to caress his muscled arm.

"Then hop on," he said leaning down.

"Um, I can't. Not in this dress. Unless you want all of those people on the deck to see my lacy panties," she whispered.

Her words had the desired effect she had hoped they would. As realization dawned on his face, he swallowed hard.

"Is that all you have on under that dress?" he asked slowly, his eyes roaming up and down her body.

She slowly shook her head back and forth.

"That settles it. My house is closer than yours. That's where we're going," he said, nodding to himself.

Olivia slipped off her shoes and held them in one hand, winding her arm around Jake's. "Let's get going already," she said.

They started walking across the grassy field in the direction of Jake's truck, but the progress was slow with a barefoot Olivia.

"Grab on to my neck," Jake said finally, scooping her up in his arms, making sure her dress was tucked securely around her.

"Don't I feel like a princess," she joked, holding onto him tightly.

He carried her easily across the hilly field to his truck parked a bit further down the road than where Olivia had parked her sedan. With her still in his arms, he opened the passenger door and set her down on the seat.

Now that she was sitting still, the truck's interior seemed to spin. As Jake slid in on the other side and cranked up the truck, she tried to focus on sobering up a bit. She leaned her head back against the seat as Jake pulled onto the main road and closed her eyes so that she wouldn't get sick. Everything seemed to be moving, except for her, and it was making her nauseated.

Leaning back didn't help, so she leaned forward, resting her head on her folded arms in her lap. Jake's hand rubbed her back in a circular, comforting motion.

"Are you okay, babe?" he asked with concern.

"Not feeling too well," she managed to squeak out, really regretting how much she'd drunk in way too short of a time.

"Just relax and take deep breaths," his soothing voice told her. She attempted to do that, but now her emotions were deciding to go into overdrive, too. A few tears landed on her lap.

"I'm so sorry, Jake. I'm such a mess right now, you shouldn't have to deal with this," she said.

"Don't be sorry. I really don't mind taking care of you. We're friends, aren't we?"

For some reason, his friend reference really bothered her, but she didn't say anything.

"I'll be okay in a few minutes," she told him.

"Don't worry—I've got you, Olivia. Don't try to pretend like you feel okay, just relax." His gentle hand massaged her neck. This moment wasn't necessarily romantic, but it was the moment that she knew. She was completely falling for him, and no matter how much she told herself she wasn't going to date or have anything to do with the opposite sex, the feelings she had for Jake were too strong to deny.

Great. Just great. Her thoughts were a jumbled mess—fueled by alcohol, charged with emotions and full of the realization that she had serious feelings for someone—and they served up a lethal combination.

She leaned back again, and Jake placed a secure hand just above her knee and gave her bare leg a reassuring squeeze. To think, she was *this close* to having what was sure to be amazing sex with the hot, muscled man with his slightly too-long hair seated beside her, and she had to go and ruin it by drinking too many tequila-laden palomas.

Olivia knew that he wouldn't try anything physical with her tonight. Her behavior in the truck proved to Jake that she was too drunk for him to sleep with her and be able to face each other in the morning without regret. *Damn it.*

Jake drove her home and helped her out of the truck, picking her up again and carrying her to the porch. She rested her head against his broad chest, enjoying the moment in his arms.

"Will you come in for a few minutes?" she asked, hoping she didn't sound too eager as she unlocked the front door.

"Of course. I'm not going to toss you through the door and tell you to sleep it off. Let me take care of you a little bit," he said, kissing her hair, and she couldn't help but be secretly thrilled at the sweet, tender way he was treating her.

"If you insist," she teased.

"I most certainly do."

He slipped a secure arm around her waist and helped her inside.

"Why don't you change into something more comfortable, and I'll get you a glass of water," he said.

She nodded, and headed to her bedroom while he busied himself getting water. Thankfully, she wasn't feeling quite as drunk as she was earlier. In the truck, she'd been seriously afraid that she was going to throw up. Now, on solid ground, everything was coming into focus a little better.

Quickly stripping off her dress, she threw on a pair of shorts and a tank top. Before heading back to a waiting Jake, she hopped into her master bathroom and quickly brushed her teeth to rid the taste of tequila from her mouth. Feeling a little more in control with every passing moment, Olivia smoothed her hair and patted her cheeks with a little cold water.

"How are you feeling?" Jake asked when she emerged from her room.

"Much, much better," Olivia smiled at him as he handed her the glass of water he'd poured.

"You look like you feel better," he remarked as they sat down on the sofa.

"I think I got a little carsick, because now I don't feel nearly as terrible as I did on the way here."

"Heyyy...my driving isn't that bad, is it?" Jake teased.

"Oh no, it wasn't your driving—it was definitely my drinking," she laughed, patting his leg to reassure him.

"Can you not hold your liquor, Olivia?"

"You nailed it. I'm a happy, messy drunk and I wouldn't have it any other way," she said with a wink before adding, "but, that is one of the reasons I don't get drunk very often. I think I drank too much too fast tonight—I'm sorry you had to cut your time at the bar short."

"No need to apologize. I enjoy your company, and if I remember correctly, our plan to leave the bar had nothing to do with your being intoxicated," he said, his eyes darkening. She warmed beneath his gaze.

"Well, I hate to break it to you, but my buzz is wearing off and I'm sobering up fast. I might end up getting all uptight again," she tried to joke.

Jake leaned closer to her. "I'm glad you aren't overly drunk. Even though I would be more than willing to take care of you, if you are up for it, I'd really like to pick up where we left off earlier," he said in a husky voice as his eyes swept over the length of her.

Olivia wasn't sure what to say, but she knew what to do. Taking his face in her hands, she kissed him with certainty. Yes, she wanted to pick up where they'd left off—there was no doubt about that.

Jake took her kiss as all the answer he needed as he wrapped his arms around her, kissing her long and hard. She was mesmerized by the taste of his kiss as his strong hands ran up and down her back, pulling her as close as possible.

His lips broke away from hers and began working their way down her neck, across her collarbone and along the rise of her breasts peeking out of her tank top. The faint trace of stubble on his jaw tickled the soft, sensitive skin, making her yearn for more of his touch and his kisses.

She leaned slightly away from him, taking the hem of her shirt and quickly pulling the top over her head before tossing it to the floor and stretching back on the couch in just her lacy strapless bra and shorts. Jake looked down at her, drinking her in with a look so scorching, her breath began to quicken and her heart started to race with only his eyes on her and nothing else.

"God, you're beautiful," he murmured as he placed his hands on her knees, slowly running them up her thighs. He stopped at the hem of her shorts and massaged back down to her knees much to Olivia's disappointment. She was ready for them both to be naked.

He ran his hands up her thighs again, but instead of slow and methodical, his hands were powerful and demanding as he grabbed her shorts and snatched them down her legs. Jake took the opportunity to toss his own shirt over his head, revealing his ridiculously well sculpted chest and abs.

Olivia leaned back up into a sitting position, inches from him, forgetting about everything else but his bared body. "I just need to touch you," she explained, exploring the planes of his torso with her hands, "and kiss you," she added, kissing his neck, trailing more kisses down his chest, abs and working her way lower still. She was about to press him back against the sofa when he grabbed her wrists.

"I'm not done with you yet," he told her, his hands gliding up her arms as he pushed her shoulders back onto the sofa. Now on her back again, Olivia arched her body involuntarily as Jake slipped her strapless bra down, baring her breasts to his hungry gaze. His fingers massaged the soft, full flesh as he ran his thumbs back and forth across her taut nipples. She was panting now.

"Want more?" he asked gently.

She could barely think for all the pleasure he was causing to build within her. Olivia hadn't had an experience like this before. He was so controlled, but excited, demanding, yet sensitive to her wants and needs. It was about to drive her over the edge.

"Oh yes," she breathed, feeling emboldened as she slid her hands over his body.

He nodded, keeping eye contact with her as one of his hands left her breasts to reach between her legs and tug her panties down. She lifted her hips to help him with the process. It turned her on so much to watch him remove her clothing.

"Tell me what you want," he leaned down and whispered close to her ear, "and be specific," he added.

"I want you to touch me."

"Where?"

"You know where."

"Say it."

Olivia sighed and took his hand, placing it exactly where she wanted it. "Here," she sighed, arching against his palm cupped against her.

Jake sucked in a sharp breath as he slipped a finger inside of her. "I think I can do that," he whispered, kissing her neck even as his fingers moved. The pressure inside of her was rising to an explosive level—especially when he whispered against her neck exactly what he was about to do to her in the most descriptive sex words she'd ever heard. She could barely breathe—this was *hot*. Best sex ever, hands-down and he hadn't even unzipped his pants yet.

His lips moved down her body deliciously, sending pleasure to every nerve ending she had, but the second he knelt between her legs and touched his mouth against her, she let out a low moan and the first crashing wave of release washed over her. She came apart at the seams as he languidly kissed, licked and caressed her intimately. She wasn't sure if she could take any more, but he was relentless as he took her pleasure-racked body to the edge again and again.

Just as she was about to succumb to another intense wave of pleasure, he jumped up and slid his pants off, throwing on a condom as her legs literally shook with adrenaline and pleasure. She felt high—almost like she was having an out-of-body experience because surely nothing on earth felt this good.

"What are you doing to me?" she rasped, as he came down over her.

"What I've wanted to do since the moment I laid eyes on you," he whispered as he thrusted inside of her.

Picking up a gentle rhythm, the hot intensity mellowed into an intimate exchange as she slid her hands up and down his back, and wrapped her legs around his waist. After a few moments, the pulsing heat returned as he picked up the pace. The charged connection reached a fever pitch before finally releasing them both, and he collapsed on top of her as they both fought to catch their breaths.

She held onto him tightly, not ready for the warmth of his body to leave hers yet. Time seemed to stand still as their hearts pounded, their breaths coming in gasps. She was content with time stopping because she was pretty sure she wanted this moment to last forever.

***

The next morning, Olivia cracked one eye open a fraction of an inch. Her bedroom was still fairly dark, so she reached for her cell phone on the bedside table to check the time. The bright screen faintly illuminated the room, letting her know it was 6:30.

Good. She hadn't slept late—she'd actually woken up early. Stretching a little, she shifted onto her side at which point she simultaneously realized that she only wore a T-shirt and nothing else, and she wasn't alone. She was staring into a bare, deliciously masculine back.

The previous night's activities came rushing back—seeing Jake at Bottom's Up, leaving with him, having the best sex of her life...she allowed herself to smile for a few seconds at those memories before the weight of what she'd done fully registered with her.

He must have sensed that she was awake because he turned to face her, smiling slowly as he said in a voice thick with sleep, "Hey there."

"Umm...hi," she replied, feeling awkward now that it was the morning after.

"What time is it?"

"Still early. You can go back to sleep if you like," she said softly.

"Nah, I'm an early riser," he said and yawned before sliding an arm around her and pulling her close, nuzzling and kissing her neck as he tugged her T-shirt up.

Olivia sighed, no longer resisting how wonderful it felt to be in Jake's embrace. Awkward conversations could wait for later. She would enjoy this while she could.

After making love again, Olivia hopped in the shower as the time for her to leave for work inched closer. When she emerged from the bathroom in just a robe after drying her hair, she found a shirtless Jake in the kitchen where he was making coffee.

"Thanks so much for putting the coffee on. I drink it every day, but I have a feeling I'm going to need a few extra cups today," she told him as she pulled a couple of cups from the cabinet.

"No problem. I'm a big coffee drinker myself," he said as he poured the coffee into the pale blue cups she'd set on the counter.

"So what's your plan for the day?" she asked casually as she took the creamer out of the fridge. She poured some in her cup and stirred as she waited for his answer.

"Jake?"

"Hmm?" he asked, looking up from his cup.

"Are you alright?"

"Yes, fine. Why?"

"No reason, just checking," she said, not wanting to sound overly concerned that he had ignored her question about his plans.

Jake sighed. "Olivia, remember when I said I couldn't get involved, we'd just be friends, all of that? Even though I keep doing everything around you that says that I want to get involved with you and definitely be more than your friend?"

That was a loaded statement. It was too early and she hadn't had enough coffee to have this conversation yet.

"Yes, I suppose. I think I said the same thing," she said carefully.

"You did. The deal is this—I like you, I mean, I really like you, but I'm in the middle of something and because I really like you, I can't put you through it, too."

"Ohhhkay, thanks I guess? What are you trying to say?" Olivia asked, confused. On one hand, she was beyond thrilled that he cared about her, but on the other, this felt like a breakup.

"I'm saying that I love spending time with you, and I don't want to stop, but I can only give so much. I can't...let things go further than how they stand now, but I'm not saying that because I wouldn't want us to become more."

"I think I get it. You want to be friends with benefits," Olivia stated, remembering now why she was trying to swear off dating.

"That's not what I meant. You don't have to give me any benefits—I'd gladly just be your friend, I just can't be more than that right now."

"I want to be your friend, too. I really like hanging out with you, and you are only saying the same thing I'd initially said. I can't be mad about that. As far as benefits go, maybe we should try not to...indulge too often. Only on an 'as needed' basis," she said with a wink, trying to lighten the intense direction the conversation had taken.

"Okay, you got it. But, my 'as needed' basis is completely subjective and continually changing," he laughed.

"As is mine, sir. As is mine," she said over her shoulder as she headed back to her room, coffee in hand, to finish getting ready for work.

Olivia mulled over their conversation in the kitchen as she applied her makeup. She was glad that she and Jake were on the same page about their relationship, but she didn't like knowing that if he had said he wanted to pursue something more, she would have been on board with that, too. She also didn't like him being so evasive about his plans. It's not like she had to know where he was and what he was doing, but being secretive about it wasn't cool either.

Twenty minutes later, dressed in jeans and a bright floral top, she was ready to go. "Ready?" Jake asked her as he hopped up from where he'd been waiting for her on the sofa.

"Yep, let me just grab some coffee," she told him. "Thanks for taking me to get my car," she added.

"No need to thank me, Olivia. Do you really think I would take off this morning and leave you without a ride?"

"You've already given me one ride this morning that I absolutely must thank you for," she said with a wink, "but I could have called one of the girls at work to come pick me up, so yes, I do need to thank you for waiting to take me to my car."

"You think you're funny, don't you?" Jake asked, trying to look serious, but the corners of his mouth were tugging upward.

"Why, yes I do," she deadpanned.

Jake couldn't help but laugh.

Chapter 7

Saturday at the salon passed by in a whirlwind like it always did for Olivia. Thankfully, the steady stream of clients kept her from having to divulge details about her night with Jake. Kacie kept shooting her knowing looks from behind the reception desk, but Olivia wasn't about to go into what happened after she and Jake left the bar. She would just leave everyone to their own speculations.

As she cut, colored and styled, Olivia wasn't as talkative as usual with her clients. She was definitely distracted by her own thoughts. She'd really enjoyed being with Jake, but his slight bit of shadiness this morning was bothering her.

She'd only asked what his plans for the day were just out of polite curiosity—she wasn't angling for a date tonight or demanding to know how he spent his time. Why did he feel the need for such secrecy? Sure, she had her own secret, but she wasn't afraid to share it with him if he asked.

She shook her head at her thoughts. For someone who swore she no longer wanted to play this dating game, it sure felt like she was an active participant. There was no way she could help herself now that she was entangled. Her human nature was getting the best of her.

Olivia knew she had feelings for Jake, and the friends with benefits arrangement they'd discussed earlier was more than likely going to make things worse. She sighed. Maybe she should just avoid him for a while and clear her head—maybe that would help the feelings go away and she could just focus on their friendship and enjoying each other physically.

After finishing her last haircut of the day, she was mentally and physically drained. Olivia darted out of the salon as fast as possible to avoid Kacie cornering her about how she'd spent the previous night.

Once she arrived back home, she took a much needed afternoon nap on the sofa. When she finally opened her eyes hours later, the living room was almost completely dark. Disoriented and still sleepy, Olivia was surprised to see the sun had set and the sky was only faintly tinged with the sun's lingering pinks and golds. She'd slept the rest of her Saturday away!

She picked up her phone from the end table and saw two missed calls and a text from Jake. The text read, "Hey, just thinking about you. Call me."

Olivia hopped up and tossed the phone on the couch. She just couldn't deal with the Jake situation tonight. She didn't want to feel so excited that he'd called. Twice.

Tonight, she would do something that focused solely on her. After she ate a sandwich standing at the kitchen counter, Olivia ran a bath, adding lavender oil and dried rose petals, poured herself a generous glass of wine and settled into the tub with the mystery novel she'd been trying to read for a couple of weeks now.

An hour later, when the bath had turned too cool to enjoy anymore, she slipped out of the tub and wrapped up in her soft gray robe. Sufficiently relaxed and calm, she checked her phone and saw that Jake had called again while she was in the bath. She couldn't help smiling. A guy didn't just call a girl three times without having some serious feelings for her.

Staring down at the phone, she tried to decide whether or not to call him back, but then his little "I can't be your boyfriend" speech popped into her mind, which prompted her to just turn her phone off completely and go to bed while the lavender, wine and way too long nap this afternoon still had her feeling sleepy.

***

"I called you at least ten times last night," Jake said in greeting. Olivia's high heel had only just stepped inside the sanctuary when he'd made a beeline for her.

"Good morning to you, too, Jake," Olivia replied, feeling the eyes of several members of the church's singles group trained on her and Jake standing close in the middle of the main aisle.

"Did I do something to make you mad?" he asked, ignoring her attempt to brush him off. She took a long, hard look at him and immediately regretted it. In his chambray shirt and navy tie, slight bit of stubble and tousled hair, he was, once again, way too gorgeous.

"No, I'm not mad," she said.

"Then why didn't you answer or call me back? I realize I sound like a needy girl right now, but I was seriously worried about you. I thought we were friends."

"We are friends—nothing more, remember? I was...busy last night," she said, almost cringing because she knew it was a cheap shot.

"I think we need to sit down and really talk," Jake said, looking uncomfortable.

"Now isn't really a good time," Olivia told him, looking around as the sanctuary filled for the morning service.

"Will you go to lunch with me after church?"

"I have longstanding plans that I can't break," she said, thinking about lunch with her family at Granny Parker's house, "but what if we meet later for dinner?" she offered.

"Dinner later. That will work. Pick you up at seven?"

Olivia nodded before heading to sit with her family. Her sister was staring her down as she scooted into the pew.

"You better spill the details at lunch, girl," Katie whispered under her breath.

Oh Lord. She hadn't anticipated the family audience. Olivia clamped her lips together, preparing to spend most of the family dinner with them sealed tight. There was no way her sister or anyone else was going to get any information out of her. Sure, she knew people were speculating—especially after Friday night, and that was fine. But she wasn't even sure how to classify what was going on between her and Jake, much less share details with anyone.

To Olivia's surprise, when the service concluded, Jake hurried over to her as she attempted to vacate her family pew. Unfortunately, Lindsey and a few of her friends had one side blocked, and her parents had the other side blocked, too. She stood there looking back and forth, contemplating if escape was worth hurdling the pew in front of her. As Jake approached, treating the sanctuary like a running track seemed even more tempting.

"Hey, I just wanted to double-check our time for this evening," he started before Katie saw him with Olivia and darted across two aisles to catch him before he walked away.

"You have no idea what you have just walked into," Olivia said to Jake under her breath as Katie, all smiles, extended a hand of introduction to Jake.

"Hi there, I'm Katie Anders, Olivia's sister. It is so nice to meet you," she said in the perkiest voice imaginable.

"Jake Harper, nice to meet you, too," Jake said as he shook her hand.

"So how do you and Olivia know each other?" Katie dug right into her questions.

"He's working on a renovation for the salon," Olivia said flatly.

"Fascinating," Katie replied, looking at Jake as she said it. "So, Jake, do you have plans for lunch?"

"No, not necessarily."

"Why don't you come with us to our grandmother's for lunch? We go every Sunday as a tradition of sorts, and I know Granny has been wanting to invite you, since you are new in town and all," Katie said. Olivia's jaw was literally hanging open. What was Katie's purpose in asking Jake? Why was she so hell-bent on figuring out what was going on between the two of them?

"I suppose I can come," Jake said, looking at Olivia for a clue as how she wanted him to respond.

"Great! Well, listen guys, I've got to go get my babies from the nursery. I'll see you two at Granny's house!" Katie said enthusiastically, leaving as quickly as she'd come.

"What just happened?" Jake asked after Katie had zoomed out the door.

"You just agreed to have lunch at my grandmother's house with my entire family. I'm sure your head is about to explode."

"Why do you say that?"

"I'm pretty sure meeting a girl's entire family isn't preferred by those not looking for a commitment."

"Why are you being so crabby? I thought we were on the same page. And it isn't that I don't want a commitment, I just—"

"Save it, Jake," she cut him off. "You're right in a way—I went into this not wanting anything romantic to happen between us," she said, picking up her purse and motioning for him to follow her out of the church.

"Do you want to just ride with me? I can bring you back by here after lunch to get your truck," Olivia said once they were outside.

"That's fine."

They walked across the parking lot to her car in weighted silence. There were so many words that needed to be spoken between them, and she wasn't sure how to start.

"Just to warn you, you're going to be asked about five hundred times if you are my boyfriend. When you say we're just friends, they will ask why, as well as a hundred other inappropriate questions. Be prepared," Olivia told him when they'd settled into the car.

"That's good to know. We're still on for dinner tonight, right?"

"Yes, that's fine. I'm sorry if you think I've been short with you—I've just had a lot on my mind, and to be honest, this isn't how I saw things going between the two of us. Things always get messy when feelings are involved."

"Let's just put this conversation on pause until later, alright? I'm pretty sure we both like each other and enjoy each other's company, so during lunch, let's just focus on that," Jake said, taking Olivia's hand in his.

She considered pulling it away, but decided against it, letting it rest comfortably in his on the console.

They pulled into Granny Parker's long graveled drive and she parked the car next to her cousin's pickup truck. Letting go of Jake's hand, she checked her reflection and took a deep breath.

"Ready for this?" she asked.

"As ready as I'll ever be," Jake said with a shrug, not looking nearly as concerned as she felt the situation warranted.

As soon as they stepped onto the wide, wraparound porch, the front door swung open, and Granny Parker, still wearing her pastel Sunday suit under her floral apron, threw her arms open wide.

"Why, Jake Harper, ain't I pleased to have you here for lunch today!" she exclaimed, giving Jake a nice big hug.

"I'm pleased to be here, Mrs. Parker," he replied, a big smile on his face.

"Call me Granny—everybody does," she told him, beckoning them inside the slightly too warm house filled with the scent of fried chicken and biscuits.

Several cousins and Olivia's parents and sister were in the family room and stared as Granny Parker led the way to the kitchen.

"Do you two mind being on biscuit duty?" the elderly woman asked with a wink.

"Not at all," Olivia said. She grabbed a couple of crocheted potholders and the big bread basket with its well-worn tea towel and took a position in front of the oven as Jake tagged along.

"What do I need to do?" he asked.

"Just stand there and keep me company. It really doesn't take two people to do this, but Granny was saving you from being thrown to the wolves as soon as you stepped in the door."

When the biscuits were sufficiently golden and slightly brown on top, Olivia pulled them from the oven and Jake helped her transfer them to the waiting basket. Soon after, the large family gathered in the kitchen to say a blessing over the meal.

As her father prayed, Olivia was surprised to feel Jake's arm find its way securely around her waist, but it was definitely not unwelcome. It felt nice to be in this memory-filled kitchen, surrounded by everyone she loved, with a strong, masculine hand resting gently on her hip.

The only downside was the look her sister was giving them while they should have both had their eyes closed. Olivia saw it in Katie's face—Katie could tell they had slept together. Trying not to seem like she was turning him down, Olivia casually stepped out of

Jake's light embrace when the prayer ended, and directed them into the line quickly forming to make a plate where the food had been set up buffet-style along the kitchen counters.

Olivia spent the entire lunch and the thirty minutes they stayed to help clean up afterward avoiding her sister, just as she and Jake both dodged the "are you dating" question over and over in the same time period.

Once back inside the haven of her car, she breathed a sigh of relief. "We made it," she said to Jake.

"I actually really enjoyed being there—I love your big family, and they are so friendly, too," Jake told her as she pulled back down the drive.

"Friendly, but nosy," Olivia replied.

"Haha, true. But I think it's more like curious, genuine interest."

"Whatever you want to call it is fine, but I know your ears have got to be burning because they are surely talking up a storm about the two of us right now."

A few moments later, Olivia pulled into the basically empty church parking lot so that Jake could retrieve his truck.

"So what do you have planned this afternoon?" Jake asked her.

"Nothing really. Go home and watch a movie, maybe take a nap."

"Sounds like fun."

"Do you want to join me? You don't have to, but if you want—"

"I'd love to just hang out, Olivia. If it's alright with you, I'll just follow you to your house."

"Fine with me," she said, still unsure how to take this overly attentive Jake. It was as if he was jumping at every chance to be near her.

He leaned over and kissed her lips lightly before getting out of her car. "See you in a few," he called over his shoulder as he jogged the few steps to his truck.

When they reached her house, Olivia got out, but Jake lingered in his truck, on his phone, his brow furrowed. He was clearly in the middle of a heated call. She stood there for a second, unsure whether to go ahead and go inside or wait for him to finish talking. Jake answered her unspoken question by waving her in and holding up the "I'll just be in one second" signal. She nodded and headed indoors, ready to change out of her sundress and into something comfortable.

She changed into a pair of running shorts and a T-shirt and peered out her living room window to see that Jake was still talking on the phone. Her curiosity was now kicking into overdrive. What was so important that it warranted such a serious call on a Sunday afternoon?

A few minutes later, Jake came inside. Olivia was kicked back on the sofa, flipping through a magazine.

"I'm sorry about that," Jake said, his voice tense.

"Is everything alright?" she asked him, setting the magazine aside.

Jake paced the small space that separated the living space and dining area. The crease of his brow and the troubled look in his eyes showed his obvious distress. Olivia's stomach was in knots, but she tried to remain patient and wait for Jake to speak. Whatever he had to say seemed hard enough—he didn't need to deal with her pressing him to talk.

"Olivia, I need to tell you something. I didn't want to bring it up until I knew for sure which way things would go, but we've gotten pretty close, and it just seems wrong to continue to be...whatever we are...without coming clean."

"Okay, Jake. I hope you know you can talk to me—I want you to know that I'm your friend first before anything else."

"I believe that, I do. But this particular situation isn't an easy thing to handle. You see, I'm recently divorced. I've been separated for two years, but the divorce was officially finalized two months ago," he said.

"That's not all that terrible. I know divorces are messy, but I thought you were about to say you'd committed a crime or something," Olivia told him, trying to lighten the tense mood.

"It isn't all that terrible, but that isn't everything. I have a daughter. Her name is Emma and she's six years old. I've been a custody battle to end all custody battles with her mother. I want to bring her here to live with me because her mother is not necessarily the best influence in Emma's life right now—she's very much about partying, drinking and hopping from one rich man to another. She has a serious alcohol problem, but I have suspicions that she may have problems with drugs, too. It isn't healthy and I don't want my child involved with it," Jake explained.

"Oh my. That is...I'm sorry to hear that. I really am. I bet Emma is a really sweet girl," Olivia said when she found her voice. Her mind was reeling. Jake had a child?

"I know it's a lot to take in—I do. This custody battle has been very stressful—it's why I was absent from the job site so much this week, and Emma being in that unstable situation weighs heavily on my mind all the time."

"I can only imagine," Olivia replied. She patted the seat next to her. Jake sat down and she threw an arm over his shoulders and gave him a squeeze.

"With everything going on, I just didn't feel like it was right to get involved with someone, which is why I kept my distance from all of those women with the casseroles and the invitations. You were different—I could tell you weren't interested in a relationship, and it was so nice to be around someone without all that added pressure. But instead of it being the easy friendship I was hoping for, I ended up falling for you. Yes, I said it. I have serious feelings for you. But with everything going on with Emma and the courts, I can't focus on a relationship right now. As much as I want to," he explained in a tortured voice.

"It's okay, Jake, I promise. I would be lying if I said I didn't have feelings for you, too, but your daughter needs to come first. Let's just be friends. Nothing else. No benefits—because that makes things way too complicated. Do you think we can do that?" she asked, waiting, hoping, praying that she wouldn't completely lose him, but understanding the reason if she did.

"I want, no I need, your friendship. It's been so hard to go through this alone. My aunt and uncle know some of the story, but they are getting on up there in years, and I don't want to worry them too much. My parents are gone, and I feel like I have no one."

"That isn't true," Olivia whispered, slipping her hand into his, "you have me. I'm not going anywhere," she promised. Her heart hurt for him—how terrible to go through such a rough process all alone.

"Our final hearing is this Thursday in Atlanta, I know it's a lot to ask, but would you come with me?" he asked her.

She mentally went through her calendar for the upcoming week. Besides Thursday being her monumental thirtieth birthday, her appointments and other stuff going on could be rescheduled.

"I will come with you—I just need to rearrange a few things. When are we leaving and when are we coming back?"

"Leaving Wednesday night and if all goes to plan, I'll be awarded custody of Emma, so I'll have to get her packed up, and hopefully head back as early as possible on Friday. I think it would be good for her to have a positive female influence to help make her feel more comfortable. She hasn't been with me much in the past several months because her mother has kept her away, but we've always been very close. I know she's going to be nervous and scared because of all the changes, though," Jake worried. Olivia squeezed his hand tighter.

She hurt for him and Emma. How terrible to go through all of this! She felt honored that Jake was including her in this part of his life and truly hoped she could help Emma and be there in any way that she could for this little girl she'd never met.

"I'll be there for you and for her," Olivia said, her voice tight with emotion. She'd never bargained for this when she'd struck up a friendship with Jake a couple of weeks ago.

Chapter 8

"So a little birdie told me tomorrow is your birthday," Jake mentioned as they headed down the interstate on their way to Atlanta late Wednesday afternoon. Olivia stared out the window as they passed identical pine tree grove after pine tree grove.

It felt strange to her how she didn't care as much about her milestone birthday as she had a few weeks ago. The journey Jake was on really put things into perspective. Parties, dancing and cooking classes, while enjoyable, just didn't seem all that big of a deal anymore. She didn't even care if she had a cake—the best present ever would be Jake getting his little girl back.

Throughout the week, Jake had shown her pictures and told her stories about Emma. The lanky little girl with honey blond curls was adorable and had a twinkle in her eye in most pictures. Olivia imagined that Emma had a bit of a mischievous streak—not so terrible that she stayed in trouble, but just enough to keep her adventurous.

Despite their promise to just be friends, and even though nothing beyond holding hands had happened between them since Sunday when he'd kissed her goodbye, Olivia's feelings had only grown for Jake.

He was everything she could have ever imagined she wanted in a man and more. Kind, thoughtful, gorgeous, hilarious, big-hearted—what more could she want?

Monday, they had gone shopping for Emma's room. Olivia had helped him pick out a pale pink and aqua bed set and a little lamp with crystals dangling off it. After they'd set the room up, Jake looked around.

"Are you sure she's going to like it?" he asked. Olivia had peered at the white antique furniture, the pale pink and aqua accents, the cozy chair in the corner for reading, the bookshelf full of books, and the doll he'd gotten her that she'd propped up on the bed in front of a frilly, monogrammed pillow.

"What little girl wouldn't love this bedroom? Heck, I'd like to live in this room," she teased, pushing his shoulder.

On Tuesday they'd went to salsa class, and the fun hour proved to be the perfect distraction to all that was going on between them and Jake's custody issues.

"Yep, tomorrow I turn the big 3-0," Olivia said, snapping out of her reverie.

"I'm sorry you have to spend your birthday dealing with my crisis. If I'd known, I would have never asked you to go. It was unfair of me," he said, his eyes staring down the road.

"That's exactly why I didn't say anything. It's just a day, really—what you're heading to tackle is monumental," she pointed out.

"But still, spending a birthday waiting in a courtroom isn't anyone's idea of a good time."

They fell into a comfortable silence as the sky darkened and they headed south. Olivia was soon lulled to sleep by the steady hum of the engine as they sped through unchanging scenery.

***

"Hey, sleepyhead. We're here," Jake's voice stirred her out of the tight embrace of her dreams. She slowly opened her eyes to see that they were inside a parking deck, the garish fluorescent light harsh to her disoriented vision.

"Where is here?" she asked, stretching. She'd fallen asleep slumped against the side of the truck, and her neck was definitely protesting.

"The hotel. Do you mind sharing a room?"

"Jake, we've shared a bed. Why would I mind a room?" she asked, thoughtlessly. Her inhibitions were lowered in her still drowsy state.

"Well, because," he cleared his throat, "we're trying not to do that at this point in our relationship."

"Oh gosh! Sorry. I shouldn't have said it like that, but I really don't mind sharing a room. It would be awfully lonely if I had to have one to myself."

"I just wanted to make sure. I'd gladly pay for you to have your own if it makes you more comfortable, but I had a feeling you wouldn't have wanted that."

"You were right. What time is it?" Olivia asked as she slid her sandals on and stepped out of the truck.

"Nearly ten. The hearing starts at nine sharp, so I figured we could order room service and relax before hitting the hay."

"Sounds like a good plan to me," she replied, grabbing her overnight bag, but Jake took it from her and carried both of their bags. Even when she insisted on carrying it, he wouldn't hear of it.

They entered the lobby of the boutique-style hotel and Olivia took in the surroundings. The space was warm and polished, but dark and edgy at the same time with its rich wood beams, concrete floors and burnt-orange velvet chairs. The whole place screamed sumptuous and expensive.

"This is a really nice hotel for such a serious visit—I was expecting something along the lines of the Holiday Inn," Olivia muttered to Jake as they entered the stainless steel elevator.

Jake laughed. "I know we haven't known each other very long, but what about me says that I would take you to a Holiday Inn?"

"Well, it's not like a date or a romantic thing..."

"But isn't it your birthday tomorrow?"

"Yeah, but that doesn't warrant staying somewhere so—"

"Yes, it does," Jake cut her off, taking her hand in his, "you deserve more than this. You deserve anything you want, Olivia. I don't think you realize how amazing a person you are. I know this isn't a 'fun' trip, but once I found out tomorrow is your birthday, I tried to make this trip at least a little bit of a celebration for you."

"The celebration I want more than anything else is for you to carry your daughter out of that courthouse tomorrow," Olivia told him, her voice ringing with the sincerity she felt deep in her bones.

Jake leaned down and kissed her softly on the lips, lingering even as the elevator doors opened onto the top floor.

"I know we aren't supposed to be doing this, but I figured we could maybe make an exception since it's your birthday and everything..." Jake trailed off as he lifted his face away from hers and took their bags into the penthouse suite.

"Hmm...an exception sounds intriguing. But tonight isn't my birthday. I don't officially turn thirty until tomorrow evening at 8:47," she pointed out as she followed him.

"Close enough, don't you think?" he asked as he dropped their bags just inside the door to the bedroom of the suite. Olivia half heard him as she was busy taking in the luxe beauty surrounding her. Fawn leather chairs and linen panels, steel and marble accent tables, sea glass vases and the funkiest bright green rug that she'd ever seen made up the living area. Just through a doorway, a large king-size upholstered bed was made up in several shades of gray. Stark white curtain panels opened to the twinkling lights and cityscape of Atlanta.

However, what really captured her attention was the bathroom that housed a large, modern spa tub—the wall between the bathroom and bedroom was completely made of glass and the tub felt as if it was in the bedroom but it wasn't.

"Have you seen this tub?" Olivia called out to Jake who was still in the living area. He came up behind her and slid his arm around her waist.

"I think we need to test it out," he whispered against her hair.

"Okay, but I have one condition. Did you bring your swimsuit?"

"We are, in fact, adults and not five-year-olds—you do know that, don't you?"

"Jake, as much as I would like to start this evening in that tub with you and continue into the bed...or the sofa...or the floor...heck, even against the wall..." her eyes glazed over for a second as all the possibilities played out in her mind.

"You were saying," Jake said, taking the opportunity to pull her into his arms and kiss along her jaw. She shook her head, hoping to clear the overwhelming desire starting to take over.

"I was saying that we shouldn't. Despite wanting it, it isn't right. You're in the middle of something huge right now, and we are in a good place. Most of the time, if sex gets involved, people can't just be friends. We're lucky that we are able to be such good friends after sleeping together, and I don't want to jeopardize that."

Jake contemplated her words carefully before taking her face in his hands and gazing into her eyes. "On one hand, I agree with you—I not only enjoy our friendship, I need it. You came into my life at a moment when I needed someone to make me smile— to enjoy life again after having to leave my daughter to get settled in Morning Glory. I know others tried to make a place in my life, but didn't—you were just you—no fronts, no facades, just simply you. And for some reason, all I wanted to do was get to know who you were and what your beautiful, hilarious, determined self was all about.

"The point I'm trying to make is this—I want us to be friends, of course, but I don't want us to just be friends and that's it. You are so much more to me than that. I only said what I said this past weekend because it is crucial that Emma is my main priority and that I focus fully on her. But this week, you've somehow made her, my Emma, this little girl that you've never even met before, your main priority, too. You have been fully focusing your energy on what could happen tomorrow. I didn't ask you to do that, and I certainly didn't expect it, but here you are, in Atlanta, about to spend your birthday at a court hearing because you want to be there for me and for my little girl.

"How could I not fall for someone so sincere and as beautiful on the inside as she is on the outside? I can't resist you, Olivia, and I don't want to," he told her before capturing her lips with his. She melted into his kiss—warmed not only by the hard planes of his body pressed against her, but also by the sweet, tender words he'd just said to her. Never in her life had someone been so candid with her about what she meant to them. He was detailed, he was thorough, and he, most importantly, was sincere. Now, more than ever before, she knew that she was a goner. Whatever happened after this, Jake Harper held her heart in his hands. She was head over heels for him.

Breaking her lips away from his, Olivia implored him with her expression. "I've fallen for you, too, Jake. You mean the world to me and despite trying so hard to keep you at a distance, it was impossible not to let such a good, strong, thoughtful, well-dressed man into my heart," she winked at him before finding his lips again.

"Now what was that about my swimsuit?" Jake half joked as he lifted his lips from hers and led her into the bathroom to start the tub.

Though the night was filled with bubble baths and wine, tender moments of lovemaking intermingled with wild and hot sex acts, the morning came far too soon. As the alarm buzzed obnoxiously, Olivia burrowed into Jake's chest, nuzzling her nose against the curve of his pectoral muscle.

"Good morning, sunshine," his husky morning voice half whispered in the pale morning light that filtered through the east-facing windows.

"Mmmm," Olivia managed to half say. She was so tired, her body felt like jelly and she was quite certain she couldn't move.

"Did I wear out the birthday girl last night?" he asked, his voice having the slightest hint of tease as his hand roamed down her bare back before cupping her bottom. Despite her exhausted state, certain parts of her perked right up.

"Nah, I'm awake and definitely in need of birthday sex," she said, much more alert now as she kissed his chest and shoulder, pushing her body against him as she felt his member pressing firmly into her stomach.

"I feel like I can give you that," he said, shifting her on top of him.

"I'm feeling that you can too," Olivia teased, clasping her hand around his hardness. The jokes soon ended as the intensity of the heated moment took over. Jake's hands were all over her body, caressing every inch that he could, finally settling on taking her breasts into his hands when she leaned up and took him inside of her.

As she sat astride him, she began a gentle rhythm, going backward and forward, but the pace quickly picked up as the sweet pressure of pleasure built within her. She leaned forward, her hands pressed into his chest as he took her hips in his hands, guiding her movements, dipping her down, thrusting up as he took the lead.

"Ohhh," she moaned, "this is how I should be woken up every morning," she said just before she started to pant. Seconds later, she shouted as she found her release in wild abandon, flopping onto his chest as her heart raced. He shifted her jelly-like limbs and turned so that he was now on top of her, and began to powerfully thrust into her as she pressed her hands against the upholstered headboard. Another earth-shattering orgasm soon had her arching her back and clamping her legs around him as he found his own release.

"Time to get going," Olivia murmured as she playfully smacked Jake's butt. She was feeling both energized and exhausted at the same time—good sex had a way of doing that to a girl.

"You're right," Jake said, hopping up. She watched his nude form head into the bathroom. Seconds later, she heard the shower turn on. While she waited for her turn, she pulled the Egyptian cotton sheet over her naked body and grabbed her phone off the nightstand.

Forty minutes later, dressed in a subdued pair of black pants and a pale peach blouse, Olivia gathered her bag and purse. She watched as Jake fidgeted with his tie. She could tell that the reality of what he was going to do was starting to fully set in for him.

"Nervous?" she asked, walking over to him and rubbing his arm.

"Beyond nervous. Today is the day. I feel like things will work out in my favor, but there's still that little bit of worry that I'll walk out of there defeated."

"Don't think like that. Let's pray that today goes the way that it should. That everything works out for the best for you and most importantly, for Emma," she said as she took his hand in hers and squeezed it reassuringly.

Jake squared his shoulders. "Okay, let's do this."

They took the elevator down to the lobby and walked out of the revolving glass door and into the bright morning sunshine. The courthouse was only a short walk away.

"Whew, it is hot out here to be so early," Olivia said, fanning herself in the humid air as the sun beat down relentlessly. She was used to the slight reprieve from summer heat thanks to the cool North Carolina mountain air.

"Yep. One of the reasons I moved to Morning Glory, no joke."

"I believe it," she replied as they took the steep steps up to the courthouse doors. They hurried inside and went through the screening process before making their way to a small courtroom on the third floor. Taking a seat on the wooden, pew-like bench outside the paneled door, Olivia patted Jake's leg as he shifted nervously.

"Where's Emma and her mother?" she asked.

"Her mother will be here any minute, I hope. Emma's grandmother is bringing her after the hearing starts, and they will be waiting out here. That courtroom is no place for her. As mad as her mother makes me, I don't want Emma to hear bad stuff about her."

"You're a good man, Jake."

Olivia looked down the hall at the sound of obnoxious high heels coming their way. She knew immediately that she was looking at Jake's ex-wife. The woman had a willowy frame and long brown hair, and she was wearing a black dress that was too tight and heels that were too high. She looked as if she was once strikingly beautiful, but now a hard, jaded look made it impossible to classify her as that.

"I can't believe you are doing this," the woman said when she stopped in front of Jake and Olivia.

"Olivia, this is my ex-wife, Alyssa. Alyssa, this is Olivia," Jake said, introducing the two women. Olivia nodded her head slightly in greeting, but Alyssa didn't even look at her.

"Seriously, Jake. Why are you wasting your time? You know Emma belongs with me."

"I'm not going into this here. The judge will decide what is best for her, but you and I both know that it isn't you."

Alyssa stalked to the other bench a few feet away and sat down in a huff. Soon after Jake's and Alyssa's attorneys arrived to brief them, and before she knew what had happened, Olivia was standing at the back of a courtroom as a judge in a flowing black robe entered to preside over his court.

Her stomach was in knots and she bit her fingernails, a habit she hadn't given into in more than a decade, as the judge went over the evidence, listened to the attorneys presenting their cases one last time, and took final statements from Jake and Alyssa.

Finally, the bailiff rose, and announced, "This court will take a one-hour recess for lunch while the judge decides his verdict. Be back promptly at 1:15."

Jake stood and hurried down the center aisle to Olivia's spot at the back. "Now all we do is wait," he said, relief and worry both present in his voice.

***

"All rise for the Honorable Judge McAllister presiding. This court is now in session," the bailiff called out. Olivia stood at once, but it felt like her stomach stayed on the bench. She gripped the bench in front of her to steady her nerves.

"You may be seated," the judge announced. "I'll be quick about this. After sifting through all evidence and listening to your sound testimonies, I have full confidence in honoring Mr. Harper's request for sole custody of Emma Anne Harper effective immediately. Ms. Harper, upon reflection, I suggest that you seek counsel for your addictions. After a sixty-day probationary period, we will revisit the length and breadth of your visitation rights, but for now, you may visit Emma every other Sunday for a four-hour supervised visit if you so choose." And with that, he wrapped his gavel and everything was over.

Jake turned around, and Olivia's heart soared as she took in the biggest smile she'd ever seen on his face. She smiled back at him and motioned for him to hurry out the door to his daughter. He nodded, looking nearly giddy as he rushed by her. She followed him out and was so blessed to witness the moment he took his daughter into his arms.

The curly-haired girl's arms wrapped tightly around his neck as she squealed, "Daddy!"

Jake picked her up and twirled her around, overcome with emotion. Olivia feared she was becoming a blubbering mess as she saw tears trailing down the side of Jake's face.

"Am I going to live with you now, Daddy?" Emma leaned up from Jake's shoulder to ask him.

"Yes, sweetie. You are going to be with me now," he said, smoothing a wayward curl out of her face.

Olivia had it sort of together until she saw Emma's face light up with sheer happiness to the point of tears at finding out she would be living with her dad. Witnessing that precious moment was too much for her and a low sob escaped her lips.

Jake turned around to face her and waved an arm, beckoning her over to Emma and him. Olivia made her way to them, wiping her tears the best she could with the backs of her hands.

"Emma, this is Olivia, a kind, beautiful, loving lady that means very much to me. She is going to be a big part of your life. Olivia, this is my darling Emma that I've told you so much about," he said as he stared at the profile of his daughter as she took in Olivia.

"Hello, Emma. It's so very nice to meet you," she said, extending her hand to the little girl shyly staring at her. Emma looked at Olivia's hand, then back up to her face, contemplating what she should do.

Olivia placed the hand she had extended onto Emma's shoulder and gave it a squeeze. "I know there's a lot going on right now. Don't worry about me—focus on your daddy. I'm so happy that the two of you will be together now—he loves you so much and has missed you terribly."

Emma burst into a grin at Olivia's words. Olivia knew better than to push the little girl. Emma's entire life was changing, and she wanted to make it as easy a transition as possible for her. She knew she would be whatever Emma needed her to be, and right now, that was just support without expecting anything in return.

***

"Are we all packed up and ready to go?" Jake asked as he came back into the hotel room from getting donuts and bagels for the girls Friday morning.

"Yep," Olivia said, smoothing Emma's hair into a ponytail. She and Emma were now fast friends and it had only been a day. Olivia had been able to make progress through her career knowledge of all things. Emma's favorite game to play was beauty shop, and she adored Olivia for her wealth of information, constantly plying her with questions that Olivia happily answered.

"Daddy, are we going home?"

"Yes, Emma. We are going to our new home. You've never been there before, but I think you are going to like it very much."

"Will Olivia be there?"

Jake met Olivia's eyes before replying. "Olivia has her own house, but she will be visiting us and we will be visiting her all the time."

"Good. I really like her," Emma said, not paying attention to the fact that Olivia was standing a few feet behind her.

"Me too, Emma girl. Me too," Jake said, smiling at Olivia.

A little later in the parking deck, after getting Emma situated in her booster seat, Jake pulled Olivia to the side. "I just want to say, you are amazing. I can't wait to start this journey together—not only because of our friendship, and the awesome role model you are for my daughter, but because I'm falling in love with you. I know this is a parking deck and I don't have a dozen roses or violins playing, but I do have this," he said, reaching into the truck and pulling out a slim white box.

Unable to speak just yet, Olivia took the box from him. "It's your birthday present," he told her as she untied the satin ribbon and opened the lid. Nestled on a bed of soft linen, an engraved silver bracelet shone in the sunlight. She picked up the bangle and read out loud the words etched into it, "The best is yet to come."

"I believe that with all my heart. I can't wait to get back to Morning Glory, settle into a pattern with you and Emma as I learn and get to know the two most important women in my life."

"Jake, this is perfect," she said putting the bracelet on her wrist. "I never imagined even a month ago that I would be here in this moment with you, but I am so happy that I am. It's exactly where I belong— with a man I'm head over heels for and his daughter that has captured my heart, as well." She kissed his lips and took his hand.

"Let's go home," he said.

"I already feel like I'm there," she replied, resting her head against his shoulder.

What to read next?

If you liked this book, you will also like *Priceless Love*.
Another interesting book is *Investment in Love*.

Priceless Love

Miranda has an amazing job on a seven-star cruise ship, her best friend works with her and she gets to sail around the world. But her perfect world she tried so hard to create comes crashing down when Alec Bane climbs on board. He is rich, handsome and a complete playboy. From the minute he sets eyes on Miranda he singles her out, but Miranda won't be fooled by his charming manners and alluring dark blue eyes. She sees him for the womanizing fool he is and won't have anything to do with him. Fate however has something else in store for her. When she is outsourced to another company, Miranda finds herself working as a personal assistant for Alec Bane. Seeing him every day and being in such close proximity has a strange effect on Miranda and she doesn't know how long she can fight off this growing attraction. When the truth comes out about Alec, Miranda is heartbroken but gets a chance to become the happiest woman on earth.

Investment in Love

Calvin Barnard is a hard-working New York stockbroker, focused entirely on his job. His life is simple until the day he gets a call from the lawyer of his late Great-Aunt Loretta. The great-aunt he barely knew has left him $10 million and a house in the tiny backwoods Oregon town of Carterville—but there's one condition. Before Calvin can get the money, he has three months to marry a girl from that same rural town. Suddenly, everything is complicated, as Calvin tries to figure out how his reclusive great-aunt had millions of dollars, what he's going to do with her old dusty mansion, and which small-town girl will be willing to marry him on short notice. Interior designer Ellie Parker looks like the perfect solution to his problems: She's beautiful, single, and available to fix up the old house. But when Calvin starts to feel more than sympathy for sweet Ellie, he'll have to decide between the inheritance of a lifetime or the love of the most enchanting woman he's ever met.

About Emily Walters

Emily Walters lives in California with her beloved husband, three daughters, and two dogs. She began writing after high school, but it took her ten long years of writing for newspapers and magazines until she realized that fiction is her real passion. Emily likes to create a mental movie in her reader's mind about charismatic characters, their passionate relationships and interesting adventures. When she isn't writing romantic stories, she can be found reading a fiction book, jogging, or traveling with her family. She loves Starbucks, Matt Damon and Argentinian tango.

One Last Thing…

If you believe that *Priceless Love* is worth sharing, would you spend a minute to let your friends know about it?

If this book lets them have a great time, they will be enormously grateful to you – as will I.

Emily

www.EmilyWaltersBooks.com